JOSH
AND THE SKELETON

JOSH
AND THE SKELETON

CHRISTMAS EVE DISCOVERY

SKIP ASHWORTH

ARPress
45 Dan Road Suite 36
Canton MA 02021
Hotline: 1(888) 821-0229
Fax: 1(508) 545-7580

Ordering Information:
Quantity Sales. Special discounts are available on quantity purchases by corporations, associations, and others. For details, contact the publisher at the address above.

Printed in the United States of America.

ISBN-13   Softcover   979-8-89330-283-7
                eBook   979-8-89330-282-0

Library of Congress Control Number: 2024901465

I don't believe in ghosts, but after sixty-some years I believe that the spirits of difficult things are never really buried once and for all on this side of eternity.

Touches the Sky
James Calvin Schaap

CHAPTER 1

Josh stayed a long time in the hot shower, hoping to wash away the sight he saw earlier that morning. The ghost-white steam rose above the plastic sky-blue shower curtain and silver metal rod. Maybe the hot water would dissolve the gruesome picture flashing on and off in his head like the images of a video game and the heavy soapy lather would clean it all away from his memory.

The young, part-Cheyenne boy knew, however, that he saw the crow recently in a dream. The big black bird messenger warned him to avoid the old Cheyenne campground not far from his grandparents' aging farmhouse. His grandparents always admonished him to stay away from the place of the past.

When the crow appeared in his dream a few weeks earlier, a ghost lurked behind the sacred messenger. Josh recognized the area where the crow was. The place was the same snow-covered red rock ravine that he'd been to that morning. In the dream, the crow sat at the top of a large sycamore tree like the one where he saw the abandoned truck.

The eleven-year-old boy knew from stories that his grandpa Left Alone told him that the ghost, mistai, meant a dead body was somewhere in the old campground and had not been properly buried.

Many times, Josh's grandpa told stories to scare him, especially when they were in the woods. His grandpa related how ghosts made the Cheyenne feel uneasy, whose spirits came from the dead. If the corpse was not quickly disposed of, the Cheyenne believed that its ghost would not start the journey to the Milky Way until the body was put in its final resting place outside the tribe's camp. The old, craggy-faced elder also revealed how ghosts liked company for their journey, especially children, and sometimes would attempt to take the spirit of a living person with them, which meant someone would die if the body was not put to rest promptly.

Josh ignored the messenger in his dream until now. The old legend wasn't funny any longer. The crow had brought him a message, but what did it mean? Was it a warning to stay away from the old campground, or was he supposed to find the skeleton? Either way, he saw the skeleton and did not obey the forewarning conveyed in his dream. What was he going to do now?

CHAPTER 2

The night before Christmas Eve brought a heavy snowfall. The countryside was smoother and brighter than any of Gramma's cleanest sheets. No one else was up. The weathered farmhouse had that eerie early morning twilight silence. The energetic, stocky boy dressed quickly and stepped quietly down the old wooden stairs, trying not to let them creak and squeak. No need to wake up Gramma or his sister, Caroline, who his grandpa called Rosebud.

Flash, the family farm dog, met him at the back door. The Australian shepherd's tail wagged continuously like a metronome while trying to jump up and lick Josh's round face. Not succeeding, the rambunctious dog resigned himself to nipping at the heels of Josh's boots.

Slowly the electrified boy pushed open the back door, not making any noise. Flash squeezed out at the first sign of a crease in the door opening. He sprinted ahead of Josh to the backyard toward the ravine, hoping to catch unsuspecting birds or squirrels by the creek.

"Hold on, Flash!" shouted the animated boy. "We've got plenty of time."

But Flash, the blue merle sheepdog, scurried ahead, looking like a dolphin diving in and out of white caps. Josh's hair was the same color as the coal-black spots on Flash's coat. Amazed at all the snow, Josh just stood there watching Flash bark and chase falling snowflakes, leaping high in the air, attempting to catch them before they hit the swirling snowdrifts. Meanwhile, Josh tried to catch the big, wet snowflakes on his tongue. The snow was deep and beginning to drift. Josh ran after Flash the best his short legs would carry him across the snow-blown fields.

"Dang, Flash, it's cold out here. The wind cuts right through me, but this is too much fun to go back inside. Besides, we may never see this kind of snowstorm in Oklahoma on Christmas Eve again." The sheer exhilaration from falling snow kept the excited boy and his dog moving. He and Flash were the first to place their footprints on the newly fallen snow. "Isn't this great, Flash?" Flash barked his agreement.

From time to time, the red-cheeked boy would dive into a snowdrift, and Flash would dart back after him to see what he was doing, circling, and barking at him.

"Oh, settle down, boy. We'll get to the creek soon enough!" Josh yelled at his shaggy companion. Anyone watching saw quite a sight with the two of them carrying on like they were. *This is more fun* than the midway at the county fair, thought Josh, picking himself up from a snowdrift and brushing off the wet snow.

Josh hadn't been down in the ravine and along the creek ever since his grandpa went into the hospital just before Thanksgiving. Josh and his family visited the aging patriarch every evening. Josh and his grandpa spent a lot of time together and developed a strong bond. As a young child, he enjoyed listening to his grandpa tell the old Cheyenne stories and tales, passing along the beliefs of their ancestors, including the mischief of Wihio, a trickster like the coyote, and Sweet Medicine, the hero. The inquisitive boy knew that when Cheyenne related a story, they considered it a sacred act. Grandpa felt things, as did Josh. Josh had the makings of a mystic. He saw and had dreams and visions just like his grandpa.

During the Thanksgiving holidays, he worried about his grandpa and he wondered if he would ever return home again. Whenever he asked the grown-ups, they would never really answer his questions. His uncle and aunts just said that Grandpa would bounce back soon enough, but then they would go off and whisper with serious looks on their brown, creased faces. Grown-ups acted like that. They didn't think kids noticed the subtle behaviors of adults, but they did.

Josh thought he saw tears in Gram's eyes on Thanksgiving Day when they all prayed for Grandpa's recovery. Maybe the adults did believe Grandpa would bounce back like he always did. But not this time, because a week after Thanksgiving, his grandpa passed away.

Until now, Josh wasn't interested in going outside. When Grandpa was alive, the three of them—Grandpa, Josh, and Flash—went exploring to see what they could see and what Mother Earth had in store for them. Since Grandpa died, he didn't care to go because it reminded him of the good times with Grandpa that he missed.

Today was different, however, with the excitement of the cotton-white blanket of new snow. The two explorers raced along the creek and into the ravine. The familiar caw of a crow sounded in the distance, and the two of them went on their way in pursuit of the unknown.

CHAPTER 3

The gurgling sound of slow-running water down below carried up the ravine as the wind blew toward the two buddies while they moved deeper into the white and red ravine.

"Caw, Caw," called an agitated crow from high above as the snow began to lighten up and transform into a blustery flurry. The large black bird gliding above in a dance with the swirling, blowing snow flurry created a curious fantasy world, causing Josh to stare and ask, "Is this a dream or real, Flash?" Flash locked in on the crow and jumped in vain to catch the trickster in the sky. The dream bird paid no heed and only cawed louder as if laughing at the two of them, leaving Josh to wonder what it all meant. People called his grandpa a mystic, but he never heard him talk about it. Josh wondered if he was having a mystic vision himself.

The two sojourners trudged through the snowdrifts and down the slippery slopes toward where they heard the gurgling. When they arrived at the part of the creek where the water ran over black, blue, gray, and red stones, Flash gingerly crept to the edge, lowering his head for a drink. The water barely moved over the smooth stones but dropped off into a small blue-gray pool below, making a smacking sound. The clean water sparkled and glittered as it moved in, out, and over red, black, and white speckled stones farther downstream. The icy water meandered over clumps of gnarled cottonwood roots and broken remnants of Osage orange limbs like a slithering milk snake.

Josh reveled in the cedar chest smell of red cedar that filled the air and the glistening shine of the slow-moving creek. With the sounds of nature surrounding him and thoughts of his grandpa, time passed quicker than he realized. They approached a smaller replica of the larger canyon that was farther south and west from his grandparents' farm.

Sun and blue-sky patches emerged behind the two of them in the east. Small dripping icicles formed as snow melted. As the light hit them, the icy daggers shimmered like sunlight on a distant lake. The tall cottonwood and sycamore trees kept the brightness of the sun from hurting Josh's eyes. Rays of sunlight cascaded through the leafless winter limbs, covered with heavy wet snow, creating spires of light like that of cathedral steeples.

Josh packed a few snowballs and threw them at trees. "Ready, aim, fire! Gotta another one," he called to Flash. Occasionally, the animated dog darted after one of the exploding white missiles.

"Caw, Caw," mocked the crow in a nearby sycamore tree. While the big black bird rubbed its long, large black beak on a snowy branch of the scaly tree, Josh turned to see where the sound came from, but he froze at 180 degrees when he heard the whistling sound a little farther up in the ravine.

"Did you hear that, Flash? Those pine boughs are not moving." He first thought the sound was the wind blowing through the short pine trees and scrub oak lining the ravine's floor. Flash stopped for a minute, looking in Josh's direction.

"Dang!" Josh exclaimed as a chill and shiver went through him with another eerie noise, mixing with the whistling. "What's going on, Flash?"

The whistling and noises stopped as Josh made and heaved a larger snowball. He pretended to throw a grenade. That's when he saw the old Ford pickup truck wedged between an old sycamore and cottonwood tree at the bottom of the ravine. The distance was only two hundred feet away from him. Flash moved quickly toward the abandoned truck.

"Wait, Flash!" yelled Josh. Flash obeyed, but his wolflike eyes remained riveted in the direction of the truck. His ears stood at attention, and Josh gulped hard, trying to catch his breath. "What's that, boy?"

Flash barked but didn't look back at his master.

"I don't remember seeing that truck there before now."

Flash's curiosity finally took over and sprinted toward the snow-covered blue pickup. The door windows were down, and the front windshield was shattered into a sea- green mosaic of a thousand pieces.

The sheep dog investigated the abandoned truck, circling it several times, barking and jumping up and down. As Josh moved toward the truck, the whistling and bizarre noises started up again as he approached the mysterious vehicle. Confused and concerned, the generally carefree boy stopped and looked around at his surroundings.

Nothing appeared out of the ordinary other than the occasional whistling and eerie noises; the crow, sitting on the top of the sycamore tree, which was not unusual except for his dream earlier; and the mangled blue pickup truck. The truck didn't look abandoned. Josh observed dents and scrapes along the side panels of the late model truck from hitting trees, bushes, and rocks on its plunge into the ravine.

When the whistling and spooky noises stopped, Josh circled the truck with Flash nipping at the bottom of his legs where his jeans hit the snow and were wet. Josh moved sideways and shuffled snow with his feet, which were numb. As he did, Flash continued to nip at his feet.

"Stop it, Flash," pleaded Josh. "I feel like my heart's going to jump right out of my body."

Josh went to the driver's side. "Holy moly!" he exclaimed, jumping back and almost falling into the snow. "Is that what I think it is, Flash? Is that a bone hanging out of the window?" Flash stood still like a frozen snow statue.

Mustering up courage, Josh made his way closer to the truck and stopped where a ten-inch bone protruded out of the truck. Flash's barking grew more intense and agitated. Josh gagged and almost threw up when he saw the skeleton sitting behind the steering wheel, but he held back the urge with both hands covering his mouth. His head lurched forward a few times like a frog catching insects on a pond as if something was going to come out, but it never did.

CHAPTER 4

Frozen like one of the hanging icicles, Josh stood staring at the remains of some former human being, struggling to make sense out of the scene before him. Flash barked and tugged at the bottom of Josh's soaked dark-blue jeans. "What?" Josh snapped.

Josh pivoted and sprinted back down the snow-covered ravine with specks of red still visible, and Flash chasing behind, yelping as he went. Flash caught up to Josh and bolted ahead of him. Perplexed and frightened, Josh finally spoke, "Flash, wait for me." The spooked dog kept moving up the slippery ravine like a jackrabbit running from a coyote.

Breathing heavily, Josh paused to catch his breath. "Stop, Flash. I need to rest a minute." Josh thought about his dream from a few nights earlier.

Flash obeyed and returned to where Josh stood. "I had a dream, Flash, about seeing the crow and a ghost."

Flash's ears perked up as if he understood. "I should've listened to the message of the crow like Grandpa cautioned me in his stories from the past. He always told me to heed the warnings sent in a dream or vision. They're not to be taken lightly." With the excitement of the winter wonderland of newly fallen snow and brisk air, Josh lost track of how far they went into the ravine. "We should've stopped before the old Cheyenne campground, and then we wouldn't know about the…skeleton." His grandparents told him never to go in there, and now he had.

The wind blew stronger above the ravine. "That old northerner is kicking up again, Flash," commented Josh. "We better get going before it gets worse."

Above them, he could see the old oak trees at the edge of the ravine swaying to the south. With the wind came the whistling and unnerving noises of before, bringing to the frightened boy's mind the stories about ghosts making their presence known with such sounds in dark places, especially in wooded areas.

Josh, the extrovert that he was, thought out loud, "Is the dead person's ghost still in this ravine, Flash, looking for someone to take with him on his journey to the Milky Way like Grandpa used to say?" Even worse, his grandpa told him the ghosts looked to capture the spirit of a living person, especially a young person who hadn't listened to the message of the crow in a dream.

"More snow's coming, Flash. The clouds are turning gray. We gotta get out of here." They both took off running like kids on the playground to the water fountain after recess in the hot sun.

Flash charged out in front with Josh lagging behind. Josh, never really a fast runner with his bowlegs, felt like they were in quicksand, trying to run through the snowdrifts and up the slick ravine. He turned to ascend the side of the ravine, hoping to save some time. Surely his gramma and sister were up by now. Flash peered down at the winded boy and barked at him.

"Quit, Flash! I'm going as fast as I can."

The climb was harder than he expected with the wet snow. He kept slipping, one forward and two backward. The cottonwoods and redbuds, ladened with heavy wet snow, looked like doctors after a long operation in their surgery smocks. The drooping limbs appeared like melting vanilla bean ice cream cones. The red cedars provided some color with their green boughs draped in a layer of white cotton balls.

The menacing crow returned, flying overhead, screeching, "Caw, caw," alerting the world that Josh and his four-legged constant companion were in the area.

Almost to the top of the ravine, Josh grabbed for a small fledgling pin oak. He picked it because little snow was on it, overshadowed by the other bigger trees. The weary boy pulled himself up to the edge of the snow-covered ravine. He saw the flat horizon of the rolling fields in the distance. As he finally stood up, balancing on the slippery edge, Flash barked and jumped toward him. Josh backed away and lost his balance. He rolled and slid all the way back down into the ravine. Snow flew everywhere as he whizzed by tree trunks and bushes, barely missing several of them but flattening some smaller ones. Under other circumstances, it might have been fun.

Flash pursued down the side of the ravine like his name depicted and arrived about the same time. Josh stood up and brushed snow off him. Breathing slowly and with much effort, tired and wet, Josh snapped at Flash, "Thanks a lot, buddy. Fine pal you are."

Flash whimpered as he sat beside the cold and frustrated boy.

Josh felt a slight twinge in his right ankle and took a few steps to try it out. "Geez, I've sprained my ankle, Flash."

Flash looked up and cocked his head sideways as if to consider the situation. "What's a matter, boy?"

Josh sensed the dog smelled or heard something move farther up the ravine. They both stood quiet, listening for telltale sounds. A covey of quail scattered, and something moved in the heavy ground brush. Snow flew up like a whirlybird landing.

"Whaddya think it is, Flash? We've gotta get out of here!"

CHAPTER 5

Josh heard a mixture of labored breathing and thumping. Josh's adrenaline quickened, and his cheeks flushed. Between the gushing of adrenaline and frigid air, his sprained ankle wasn't feeling all that bad. The foot still couldn't bear his full weight when he tried to stand up on it.

"I need to find a walking stick to use as a crutch, Flash. You see any under all this snow? I wish I had one of the ones Grandpa used to make."

The dog barked at Josh's question.

"I know. Gramma is going to kill me."

The labored breathing and thumping noises grew louder and more distinct as he searched the bottom of the ravine, snow covered and wet as it was. He made them out to be grunting and snorting sounds.

"C'mon, Flash. We've gotta hurry up. D'ya think they're some wild pigs up there?"

Josh knew the wild pig population was growing in Oklahoma because the farmers turned them loose when people complained about the odor and health hazard created by the large pig farms. People weren't buying as much either. He knew these critters were wild, mean, and could grow to 175 or 200 pounds, and they weren't afraid of anything, especially an injured eleven-year-old boy with short, stumpy legs like theirs, but the pigs moved a lot faster.

Josh found an old hackberry branch, but the rotted wood shattered when he put his full weight on it.

Flash moved faster now and barked louder. Josh knew whatever was up there was moving closer. He found a five-foot red cedar branch lying across an old fallen elm. That's when he saw the reddish-brown head of the wild pig staring at him from about 150 feet away with its white razor-sharp teeth protruding out from both sides of its snouted mouth.

Josh guessed this pig was about 160 pounds. The ghoulish pig stood still so Josh backpedaled, never taking his eyes off the pig. He knew that the old pickup was only about a hundred feet behind him. He worked to slow his breathing down by taking deep breaths. The adrenaline rush and the need for concentration at the moment caused him to forget about his sprained ankle. Flash held his ground.

A smaller pig, not as dark as the one in front of Josh, emerged to the left of the larger pig. When the smaller one charged Josh, the big one made his move also. Josh whirled and sprinted for the abandoned truck. Flash instinctively charged the pigs, barking and growling furiously. Both pigs went at Flash, trying to trap him in front and back, but he swirled and lunged at them. The smaller and faster of the two tried to position himself behind the raging cattle dog, slashing at Flash's hind legs, but the crazed dog jumped and plunged at both enemies. Snow flew up in every direction. Slimy red clay splattered in the mix, looking like diluted blood.

Josh scrambled into the back of the truck. "Get up here, Flash!" he yelled frantically. "Get in the truck!" Flash stayed down low, snapping at the short, hairy legs of the pigs, but they changed directions as quickly as Flash. They moved like quarter horses cutting cattle.

"Get over here, Flash!" Flash grazed the hind leg of the smaller pig with his teeth. Blood turned the snow crimson. The wounded pig retreated for a moment, leaving an opening to the pickup. Flash took it in a wild burst of speed and leaped into the back of the snow-piled truck, knocking Josh backward.

Flash licked Josh, and the exhausted boy responded, "Good dog. You did a good job, boy," while he alternated between hugging and rubbing the neck of the herding dog. Flash turned to bark at the wild pigs that banged up against the truck. Josh took snow off the top of the truck's cab and made snowballs. He packed them really tight, squeezing out the excess water to make them harder. He made a dozen and let them sit for a bit so they would crystallize; the pigs showed signs of tiring and losing interest, and that's when Josh opened fire. He rifled the white conical missiles as hard and fast as he could, like a gumball machine gone wild. Grandpa always said that his grandson had an arm. What his legs didn't have, his arm did in power.

"Take that, and that, and that."

The pigs squealed and retreated back the way they came. Josh brushed snow off one of the wheel humps in the back of the truck and sat down. Flash nudged Josh's leg with his head, and the boy leaned down and petted the dog's head.

"We did it, Flash. We did it. We whipped them old, sorry pigs."

With the excitement and action wearing off, Josh felt the cold once again. Dirty white-gray clouds with scattered patches of black began moving in, and the sun wasn't shining any longer.

"We better get going, Flash, before Gramma starts wondering where we are."

Flash hopped out, and Josh climbed out the back, using the truck's bumper as a step stool. He didn't relish the idea of landing on his sore ankle.

"It's not too bad, Flash. I won't need a walking stick after all."

Flash led the way with Josh trailing slowly behind. "I hear those whistling and ghostly noises again. Do you?"

Flash stopped and scanned the immediate area. Josh realized in the emergency of fleeing from the wild pigs he sought refuge in the back of the truck with the skeleton. Things were not what they seemed and definitely not getting any better.

Josh had no idea what time it was, but he was sure it was getting late and knew he better get home soon.

They climbed up the glazed ravine wall once again, and this time Josh made sure of his footing when they reached the top. He jogged at first, and the ankle didn't hurt much, so he ran faster, with Flash leading the way. When they arrived at the two-story white farmhouse, Josh's muscles ached from running through the high snow, and sweat beaded up on his face. His heart pounded like drums banging out rhythms at a powwow to which his grandpa would sometimes take him.

"It's good to see that old farmhouse, Flash," said Josh, which they could hardly see with the blowing, swirling snow. "Looks like a snow dome, Flash." The lights were not on downstairs yet. That surprised Josh.

"I hope Gramma's okay," wondered Josh aloud. "I thought she'd have breakfast cooking by now." He wiped his running nose with the back of his gloved hand. Staying out in the cold always made his walnut-shaped nose drip. His nose was red from rubbing it and the cold.

With the sight of familiar surroundings and the subsiding of the adrenaline rush, Josh's thoughts returned to the skeleton in the truck and his dream warning him about a ghost. Through all the excitement, he'd forgotten about the bizarre sight of the crashed pickup with the bone-dangling passenger.

"We need to get inside, Flash, before Gramma and Caroline come downstairs and we're nowhere to be found." But the confused boy stood rigid in the same place with a host of questions swirling around in his head. Flash chased after some house sparrows and chickadees, scavenging around the ground under Gramma's birdfeeders in the backyard.

How did the truck end up in the secluded ravine and go unnoticed for so long? Is there really a ghost in the old campground, or is that just old Cheyenne myths? What should I do? Who should I tell? Will I get in trouble for being in the forbidden campground, and what does my dream with the crow mean? Am I in danger of the ghost?

Too many questions besieged the rattled youth, yet he had to decide quickly. He resolved to take a hot shower where he could think. Flash wouldn't be barking and being hyper. He knew what the right thing to do was, but would he get in trouble with his gramma? If Grandpa were alive, he would know what to do. He always knew.

Grandpa told good stories explaining with messages what needed to be done. Some old people are good that way, especially Gramps, being a Cheyenne. They always tell stories to explain the mysteries of life.

Whenever Grandpa told him a story, he began with, "Nahkohe," Cheyenne for "bear." That's what Grandpa called Josh because the bear was a symbol of independence for the Cheyenne. Grandpa knew that his grandson had to be independent in his life. The bear was also considered to be a relative of the Cheyenne, similar to an uncle, and brought good fortune, which his grandpa hoped for his young grandson.

When Grandpa called him Nahkohe, he knew either a story was coming, he was in trouble, or both.

"Let's go, Flash," called Josh, and he opened the back door with Flash scooting inside first.

CHAPTER 6

A knock on the door jolted Josh from his thoughts in the hot shower.

"Whaddya doin' in there?" pleaded Caroline. I've gotta use the potty." His spirited, redheaded little sister always bugged him at the worse possible times with questions like, "Can I play with you, go with you, and whatcha' makin'?"

Caroline did not show signs of their Cheyenne heritage like he did. She took after Gramma's family more than he did. Sometimes he wondered if they were really brother and sister.

Josh decided not to say anything about what he witnessed this morning. The ankle felt better, and he walked on it with little or no noticeable limp. He figured all the Christmas Eve activities and visitors would help him block out the awful scene he saw this morning. He wished his mind were like the white fallen snow on the backfields— clean, pure, and smooth. Hopefully the unpleasant sight of the lone skeleton would evaporate with the opening of Christmas gifts and festivities like early morning dew with the rising of the sun. The anxious boy looked forward to finding a new .22 rifle under the Christmas tree. That was the only thing he requested and really wanted. He knew Gramma didn't have a lot of money to buy Christmas presents for Caroline and him. He also knew that his gramma wasn't crazy about him having a rifle, especially with Grandpa not around to teach him gun safety and watch him use it properly. Grandpa was the one who said he would give Josh a gun when he was twelve, which he almost was. He knew his sister would receive the most presents because she still believed in Santa Claus, and her presents wouldn't cost as much.

Getting rid of the whistling and spooky noises associated with the ghost was not going to be as easy. Every once in a while, he heard them like muffled, distant cries and moans. While showering, he thought he saw a ghost on the other side of the shower curtain but realized it was just a shadow of a swaying maple tree limb outside the bathroom window reflecting in the vanity mirror. The noises were probably just the wind howling outside with the snowstorm kicking up again.

"C'mon, Josh, I need to go," his sister persisted. "Gramma, tell Josh to let me use the bathroom."

"Josh, what are you doing in there?" asked his Gramma as she moved toward the stairs. "I'll have breakfast ready shortly," called the frail but spry graying, red-haired woman as she ambled down the creaking wooden stairs. Her family came over from Ireland. They all remained in New York while she was the only one who moved to Oklahoma, looking for a different and more exciting life. Oklahoma was where his gramma met his Cheyenne grandpa.

"How do pancakes sound for breakfast?"

"Fine," blurted Josh as he pushed back the shower curtain.

"Josh, I want you out now. You've had plenty of time in there, and I need you to get some firewood."

"Okay, Gramma, I'm already out," responded Josh as he wrapped a big white towel around his waist and opened the bathroom door. "Hope you didn't wet your pants," teased Josh as he jiggled the bathroom doorknob, pretending he was going back into the bathroom.

"Stop it, Josh!" shouted Caroline.

"You leave your sister alone, young man," called his gramma. "I can hear what's goin' on up there. You be nice to your little sister, or I'll have your hide."

Josh went down the hallway to his room, wondering how she always knew what he was up to even though she was downstairs. She couldn't possibly hear everything. He knew she had a big bark for a petite elderly lady, but she was the most understanding and compassionate person Josh knew.

"I'll be down in a minute, Gramma, to get that firewood."

Once again Josh caught a glimpse of the skeleton and closed his eyes to wipe the image out of his head. The whistling and foreboding noises were another story. They were more persistent, and the ghost replaced the skeleton whenever he closed his eyes. He longed to know what the message of the crow meant in his dream a couple of nights ago.

"I miss you, Grandpa," Josh said softly.

When he entered his bedroom, several slender snow-laden redbud branches scraped against the frosted windowpane of his bedroom window. The sound reminded him of kids at school learning how to play snare drums for the marching band.

He flipped the light switch on to his small and sparsely decorated bedroom. With the flash of light, the ghost vision in his head disappeared. As he moved toward his three- drawer dresser, he saw the picture of his mom. Her hair was long, straight, black, and parted neatly on the right side. She had full pretty lips forming a wide, inviting smile. He missed her but not nearly as much as he did his grandpa. Grandpa was the one who would have helped him with his problem even though he went into the forbidden campground. He would have known what the message of the crow meant in his dream a couple of nights ago.

He looked in the mirror above his dresser, but all he saw was his own image with the tussled, wet, straight black hair. He wished to see Grandpa's old brown face with penetrating brown eyes, much like his own that appeared in the mirror before him.

CHAPTER 7

"Get down here, Josh. Breakfast is ready. You can get the firewood after, and I have some other chores for you to do before you go out and play in the snow."

Good, he thought while pulling his heavy blue sweater over his wet hair. She didn't know he had been outside earlier. No one knew. He decided to go visit his grandpa's grave after doing his chores. He'd ask Grandpa what to do. His grandpa would know what to do.

"I love the smell of bacon frying," Josh called to his gramma as he hopped down the stairs two at a time to the kitchen. "I thought we were having pancakes."

"We're having both. It's Christmas Eve, so I thought I'd do something special."

The bacon popped and crackled in his gramma's old black cast-iron frying pan on top of the blue gas-flame burner. "Sounds terrific to me," responded Josh, turning the corner into the spacious kitchen.

"Put the plates out on the table, Josh."

"Sure. Can you believe it's Christmas Eve, Gramma?"

"No…"

"Christmas Eve?" said his sister as she bolted down the stairs. "It's almost Christmas."

"Yeah, no foolin'," said Josh, pulling out a chrome, green-and-gray swirled vinyl chair.

"Josh," warned his gramma, giving him a stern look. "That was quite a snowstorm we had last night."

"It sure was. It looks beautiful outside," said Josh, putting a piece of crispy brown and slightly black bacon in his mouth.

"Don't talk with food in your mouth."

"Yes, ma'am."

"Yeah, don't talk with food in your mouth," chimed in his freckle-faced sister.

"You hush, Caroline," scolded Gramma. "You tend to your own business."

"Okay," said Caroline as she shook her head, swishing her hair and raising her lips up to her impish pug nose, making a face at Josh. His eyes met her pale-blue eyes, and they locked in a staring contest.

"Are you almost done eating, Josh?" asked the feisty, fair-skinned woman of sixty as she moved about the kitchen. "Oh, Lordy, I swear you eat more each day."

Josh's grandmother looked younger than her sixty years. Everyone always commented on that fact and often thought she was Josh's mother. She always looked much younger than his grandpa when he was alive.

"You about ready to start on your chores?" she inquired impatiently. "There's a lot to be done before everyone comes over tonight."

"I know. I'm done."

Josh pushed himself away from the table and brought his dishes to the sink. "I'll get the firewood right now."

"Get enough for tonight to go into the family room fireplace. You know your cousins like a good fire on Christmas Eve."

"Is everyone still coming over with the snowstorm?"

"As far as I know, but the radio did say we might get some more tonight."

"I hope so," piped in Caroline, who finished her breakfast.

"Heavens no, Caroline," exclaimed Gramma, "or everyone won't be able to come over for Christmas Eve."

"Oh…"

"Josh, you need to take out the trash and then feed the chickens. Leave the lights on to help keep them warm."

"Can I help feed the chickens, Gramma?" asked Caroline, taking her jadeite plate over to the sink.

"No, it's too cold out just yet," said Gramma. "But Gramma—"

"I need you to help me make some pies. You can roll the dough."

"But I want to help Josh. He gets to go out in the snow."

"You can go out later when the sun is higher in the sky, and you and Josh can build a snowman."

"Thanks, Gramma," said Josh with a mild degree of disappointment in his voice. But he was glad that Gramma intervened in making his sister stay inside while he did his chores. She would slow him down, as well as be a bother.

"Now, you hush, young man," scolded Gramma. "You have all morning to play in the snow and run about with Flash. It won't hurt you to build a snowman with your sister later."

"Okay."

Caroline wasn't as agreeable.

"Pooh." Caroline sighed as she moved over to the old deep washbasin.

"There're only a few dishes to dry and put away, and then you can go upstairs and change."

"All right."

Josh finished his chores in thirty minutes and went to his grandpa's gravesite. The sky was still grayish, like it might snow again at any time.

His grandpa was buried at the south end of the family farm near the creek where the red cedars were dense. Grandpa liked the red cedars, and his face and hands began to look like their trunks before he died.

Josh sat on an old oak tree stump close to his grandfather's head stone that read:

Jonas "Left Alone" Jones

1918 – 1986
A Good Family Man and Cheyenne Mystic
Gone to be with the Great Spirit

The gray clouds began to darken in the northern sky and with the wind picking up, blew the snow into higher drifts. Josh thought the drifts looked like ocean waves he saw in pictures. He never saw any in real life having always lived and stayed in Oklahoma.

"That red cedar smell reminds me of Grandpa, Flash. It's so strong this morning it tickles my nose."

Flash chased a squirrel up a tree. He kept jumping up, trying to catch the little fur ball.

"Leave him alone, Flash," called Josh as he threw a snowball at the barking dog.

He missed Flash and knocked off some snow and bluish-green berries from the cedar tree where the squirrel took refuge.

Lost in thought, Josh daydreamed of the times he helped Grandpa mend fences and replace old cedar fence posts even though the hearty wood lasted a long time. The sweet aroma in the air reminded him of other Christmas Eves when Grandpa and he went out early in the morning and cut down their own fresh juniper tree to use for their own Christmas tree.

Grandpa always let him select which tree to cut, and if the tree was too small, too big, or not a good shape, Grandpa would ask, "Are you sure that's the one you want, Nahkohe?" The aged and weathered man would also make sure the trunk was straight because often after Gramma took the tree down, he would make a walking stick out of it. He would strip the bark off with a special knife that had a curved blade almost like a horseshoe.

Grandpa kept asking him until they found just the right one. When they did, they would cut it down and drag it to the house for the family to decorate that evening when Josh's aunts, uncles, and cousins came to celebrate Christmas as a family.

Christmas was different this year with Grandpa dying only a few weeks ago. Gramma went out and bought a tree. He worried that she might even buy an artificial one in the future. Josh offered to cut one down this year, but Gramma said no. He felt big and experienced enough to do it himself now, but Gramma wouldn't listen to his pleas. She bought this funny-looking one instead and decorated it herself. The tree looked different than the ones he and Grandpa would find. The needles were longer and not as green. The needles would stick you like a wasp bite with the stinger not quite sticking in your skin. Josh thought Gramma's tree looked old and sick, but he didn't tell her so, as not to hurt her feelings. Gramma did a lot of things differently now that Grandpa was gone. Josh thought she was trying to remove anything that reminded her of Grandpa, and that bothered him. He didn't like it when she did that. He tried to do everything possible to keep his grandpa's memory alive. He sang old Cheyenne songs to himself that his grandpa taught him. Before falling asleep at night, he would recite Cheyenne myths and stories to keep them fresh in his heart and mind.

Some slate-gray-backed junco birds rummaged through the snow, burrowing their white-and-black heads and yellow beaks into the snow, swishing their heads from side to side. They were close to the cedar trees and occasionally paused to check for danger. A couple of blue jays flew up, crying, "Jeeah, jeeah," scaring off the juncos.

Josh said a prayer for Grandpa and placed some cedar boughs on his headstone. "Christmas is different this year, Grandpa. It's not like it used to be when you were here. Gramma acts strange. I really miss you."

Cold and disappointed, Josh fought back the tears welling up in his eyes. "I have a problem and don't know what to do.

I came to seek your advice. I disobeyed Gramma and you and ignored the message of the crow in a dream."

He stopped like the juncos earlier and looked around for any signs of life. Reassured that he was alone, he continued, "I went into the old Cheyenne campground and saw a skeleton and maybe even a ghost." A whistling sound emerged from behind him in the cedar grove. A shiver went through Josh. He stood up and turned around to look at the courtly trees as they swayed back and forth.

Sitting back down, he looked up and saw the clouds moving faster above him. He knew he had to get back before the next storm came in, and Gramma would be wondering where he was.

"What should I do about the skeleton I saw in the truck? Is his ghost still on the loose, waiting to be properly buried?"

He waited a few seconds, looking around for signs of life, but did not even see any birds scurrying around the area. He continued, "Who should I tell? Will I get in trouble for finding the skeleton and being in the old campground? I know you told me to stay away from there and to heed messages I received in dreams. I need your help, Grandpa. Please tell me what to do."

A crow cawed behind him, and the anxious boy remembered some verses from a Robert Frost poem that they read recently in school:

As I went out a crow

In a low voice said, "Oh, I was looking for you."

Josh was sure that his grandpa was listening to him just as he knew tomorrow was Christmas. The answers would soon come, but it was time for him to return to the house before the new storm rumbled in and help his sister build a snowman before it did.

CHAPTER 8

"It feels great to be inside again and thaw out. My skin feels like hot chocolate going down my throat."

"Do you want some hot chocolate?" asked his grandmother as she flattened the cream-colored piecrusts into her old, blackened pie tins.

"No, thanks," Josh said, hanging his fleece-lined jean jacket on an empty peg behind the kitchen door.

"Did you enjoy your visit to Grandpa's grave?"

"Yeah. How did ya' know I went there?"

"I just knew," said Gramma with a mixture of sadness and intuition in her stonewashed denim-blue eyes.

"Gramma, that turkey sure smells good. Where's Caroline?" His grandmother decided to prepare Christmas Eve dinner after all for the family. *Maybe some things are still the same before Grandpa died*, he thought.

"She's upstairs putting on her heavy clothes to go outside. I figured you'd be home soon enough from visiting Grandpa's grave."

"I'll get her, and we'll go out and build a snowman. I thought it was going to storm again when I was at Grandpa's grave, but it looks like the sun is trying to come out now."

"That's Oklahoma for ya," she said as she checked the turkey in the oven.

"That's for sure," called Josh as he ran up the stairs.

"You be nice to your sister, young man. She thinks the world of you!"

"I know."

Once he was upstairs, he called to his sister, "Are you ready yet, queen of Sheba?"

"Don't call me that!" shouted Caroline. "I'm almost ready. I'll be right down."

Caroline's coat was evergreen green with a high black collar that she had turned up with a white scarf wrapped around it.

"You look like a mummy," teased her brother as the two unlikely looking brother and sister moved down the stairs together.

"Josh," called his grandmother, "what did I tell you?"

"All right, we're going out to the front!" yelled Josh as they turned the corner at the bottom of the stairs heading toward the extra-wide Dutch door in the front of the house.

"I don't look like a mummy," retorted Caroline. "I'll beat you outside." The two of them raced through the living room.

"Stop running in the house!" shouted Gramma. Josh let his pesky sister win.

"Stop throwing snowballs at me," cried Caroline while trying to make some of her own without much success. Josh made his from the wetter snow on the porch railing. "I'll tell Gramma." She threw her poorly made snowballs back at him that looked more like a snow shower after they left her hand. "You'll get in trouble."

"Sure, sure. I'm all worried."

Flash came around the corner of the house and chased after both of them, running in circles around them and almost knocking Caroline down as he continually jumped up to lick Caroline.

"Quit it, Flash," squealed Caroline, bending over to make another snowball. Flash nudged her, and she fell into the snow and looked like a bush. Flash kept trying to lick her as she struggled to lift herself up. "Flash!" she pleaded. "Josh, help me."

"What's the magic word?" asked her brother with amusement. "Please!"

"All right," he said as he moved toward her. "C'mon, Caroline. Let's get started building that snowman."

"What should we name him?" she asked. Her cheeks were already crispy red, but the cold did not deter her enthusiasm for playing in the swirling and gusting snow. The scene was like an old-time black-and-white Christmas movie.

She turned quickly at the sound of a chirping rosy-red cardinal swooping down to scoff up some black sunflower seeds Gramma put out earlier. The golf ball-size green, fuzzy ball on top of her hat, knitted by Gramma for her last winter, bobbed up and down. Gramma made a blue one for Josh, but he never wore his for fear of what Bobby and the other boys would say if they saw it.

Caroline's hair was almost the same color as Gramma's. You'd think Caroline was Gramma's daughter instead of granddaughter. His sister's skin color was lighter than Josh's and more like her grandmother's. Josh's mother died giving birth to Caroline, and that's why they lived with their grandmother and granddad. Josh was four when she died.

Their dad was transferred back east from Ft. Sill in Lawton after their mother died, and everyone thought it would be best for them to live with their grandparents until their dad finished his tour in the army.

In the beginning, their dad called them regularly and visited occasionally. Eventually the calls and visits became less and less until he rarely ever contacted them. The last time they heard or saw him was for Caroline's second birthday. They didn't even know where he lived now.

"C'mon, Josh. What are we going to name the snowman?" Caroline's question again brought Josh out of his fantasizing about the whereabouts of his father.

"Oh, I don't know. We haven't even built him yet."

"That's okay. I want to know who I'm making."

"All right, old Joe."

"Old Joe, who's old Joe?" asked his bossy little sister, who was so heavily dressed that she resembled a snowman herself. "I think we should call him Frosty the Snowman, like the song."

"Fine, let's start rolling up the first ball."

Josh and his sister completed building the snowman in thirty minutes, and Caroline was quite pleased with their accomplishment.

"It looks great, Josh. I'm going into the house to find Grandpa's old corncob pipe."

That didn't make Josh happy, as it made him think about Grandpa as well as his dilemma over what to do about his discovery earlier that morning. "Why do you want to do that?" asked Josh, although he knew why.

"This is Frosty the Snowman with a corncob pipe and a button nose…"

"Yeah, yeah, I know," grumbled Josh. He kicked a clump of snow they hadn't used.

"I'll get a large button, and you get two pieces of charcoal for the eyes!" Caroline shouted back as she went into the house. Her lips were chapped from the cold, and it made it hard for her to talk.

Gramma gave her an old red wool scarf to go around Frosty's neck, and Josh did his part finding some branches for his arms. A thirty-foot silver maple tree stood in the middle of the front yard, and the wind always blew off old branches. With last night's snowstorm, some blew off, and Josh used them.

Josh threw snowballs, trying to hit the maple tree, wondering who the skeleton was in the truck. *Was it a man or woman, young or old, and where were they going?* He didn't think to look for a license plate.

"I got all the stuff, Josh. Did you get the charcoal?"

"Yes," answered Josh in a monotone, less-than-enthusiastic voice.

"Help me put them on. I can't reach the eyes."

"Okay."

"Gramma is looking for a hat for Frosty, and then she'll be out."

Gramma came out carrying an old black stocking cap of Grandpa's and placed it on Frosty's head.

"You two did a fine job with Frosty. Let's sing 'Frosty the Snowman.'"

Josh rolled his eyes, and Gramma cocked her head down and to the side, giving him a look that indicated he better comply with her suggestion or else.

The three of them sang, with Flash barking and running round Frosty and them. Josh prayed none of the boys from school happened by, but otherwise he found himself enjoying the moment of togetherness and the distraction from his early morning encounter.

"Let's go inside," said Gramma. "I've warmed up some stew, and I'll make some grilled-cheese sandwiches."

"I'm ready to go inside and eat," said Josh, whose fingertips were numb, and cheeks felt like they may crack and fall off into little shattered pieces like the petals off a withered rose.

"You're always ready to eat. What about you, Caroline?"

"Yeah, I'm getting cold."

"Cold? With all those clothes on, you can hardly walk," said Josh, moving toward the front porch.

"Gramma, tell Josh to leave me alone," implored the frozen little statue in the green coat.

"Josh…"

"I just helped you make a snowman."

"So?" retorted Caroline, thrusting her bottom lip out like a frog and turning her head side to side with her shoulders hunched forward.

"Let's go inside," said Gramma, getting cold herself having only put on a sweater in her rush to go outside with her excited granddaughter.

"Have you made any apple pie yet?" asked Josh.

"No, but I made some brownies."

"Oh, they're my favorite," said Caroline, who was the first one to the house along with Flash.

CHAPTER 9

"Gramma, can I have another bowl of stew?" asked Josh as he wondered if all the uncles, aunts, and cousins would come tonight with the snowstorm.

"I swear, Josh Smith, you eat more than any boy I've ever known, including your uncles, Lyle and Bob." She blew her nose into an old rag she used instead of Kleenex.

"Do you think they and Aunt Nancy will be comin' over tonight with all this snow?"

"They better come," Caroline said while wiping her mouth off with the back of her hand. "Can I have some brownies now, Gramma?"

"Yes, but next time use your napkin to wipe off your mouth," scolded Gramma. "We've had a lot of snow, and they're predicting more tonight." She looked out the window by the old gas stove. "It's turning gray outside again."

Gramma brought the stew and brownies over to the table and sat down next to Caroline and across from Josh.

"Josh, you okay?" asked Gramma, taking a long, hard look at him as she gave him more stew.

"Yeah, I was thinking about Christmas, the snow, and what gifts I might get." Josh hoped to find a .22 rifle under the Christmas tree tomorrow morning. If Grandpa was still alive, he knew for sure he'd receive one because his grandpa promised him one for his eleventh or twelfth birthday.

Josh's birthday was four days after Christmas, and he would turn twelve. He didn't like having his birthday so close to Christmas. He seldom had birthday parties because school was out, and he didn't receive many gifts like his friends whose birthdays were at other times of the year.

"Well, I'm sure Santa Claus will surprise you with some nice gifts," said his gramma. She put her right fist under her chin and starred at him, searching for clues as to what was bothering him.

"Caw, caw," sounded a large black crow sitting on top of the small barn in the backyard.

"I wonder what's got the crows all stirred up this morning. I've heard them all morning."

"It's probably nothing," said Josh defensively.

"Howdaya know?" piped in Caroline. "How much more snow will we get?" She tried to lick frosting off the corner of her mouth with her tongue.

"I don't know for sure. I know they said on the radio our chances were seventy percent to get some more."

Caroline started to wipe the frosting off with the back of her hand. "Caroline, use your napkin, young lady."

"Oh, all right."

With the cawing of the crow, Josh returned to thoughts of the skeleton and ghost. He considered asking his uncle Bob this evening what to do about the skeleton. His uncle would not be upset with Josh going on to the old Cheyenne campground because the youngest of his grandmother's children did not put much stock in the old Cheyenne legends and myths.

Clouds rolled in from the north, moving slowly but ominously as if snow would begin falling at any minute like the final scene about to unravel in a scary movie.

"Josh, you need to feed the chickens again before the snow starts. I'll put the TV on to hear the weather report after I bathe Caroline, and then you can take yours next.

"I took a shower this morn'. Remember?"

"Oh, Lordy, but I still want you to clean up. Make sure you shut the door to the coop. I don't want any unwanted visitors getting in there with this cold spell we're having. Leave the light on also."

"Sure, it won't take me long!" Josh yelled as the door slammed behind him.

Josh returned after a few minutes outside, but before he entered the house, he heard his grandmother speaking.

"Honest to goodness, Caroline, I don't know what I'm going to do with that brother of yours."

He waited a few minutes before going into the kitchen and watched the scene inside. A big smile emerged between her two rosy cheeks, chapped from being outside, and her pale-blue eyes sparkled as she said,

"He'll be okay, Gramma. He's a great brother. Look at the snowman we built together, and he let me call him Frosty."

"Yes, dear, you're absolutely right."

Josh stepped in and chimed in, "You know it." A smirk appeared on his blue lips.

"Be careful, young man, don't get too full of yourself," said his grandmother as she and Caroline moved to the front living room where the Christmas tree was.

Josh went upstairs to the bathroom. He could hear the conversation going on downstairs between his sister and grandmother and chose to linger there, thinking about the abandoned truck and skeleton.

"Can we put the Christmas tree lights on now, Gramma? Please?"

"Why not? It's almost dark outside with all those big, old, gray clouds waiting to drop more snow on us."

He finally came down and rounded the corner as they looked out the front picture window, and a brown female cardinal with splashes of red scampered around on the snow-covered ground at the base of the snowman. They both turned to see where the what a-cheer-cheer-cheer chirping was coming from as a red male cardinal flew up and perched on one of Frosty's silver maple arms.

"Look, Gramma, the birds have come to see Frosty."

"Yeah, right," said Josh.

"They sure have. Let's give them some breadcrumbs before we clean you up for tonight. I have some cornbread crumbs left over from the turkey stuffing, and you watch your tongue, young man," scolded his grandmother.

"Sorry," apologized Josh.

"Okay, they'll like that." The three of them put on their coats, grabbed the leftover cornbread crumbs, and went out the front door to feed the birds before the snow came.

When they finished feeding the birds, the phone rang as they entered the house. Caroline ran to answer it, but she was still too short to reach the black phone on the wall. Josh went to the backyard to check the chickens one more time.

"Hurry, Gramma."

"I'm coming, dear. I'm moving as fast as these old, weary bones will go."

"Hello."

"Ma?"

"Yes, Bob, it's your mother." She always knew her youngest son's voice, and he insisted on starting out his phone conversations with her the same way.

"Howdaya know it's me?"

"I just know, Bob. You're my son."

"Have you been listening to the weather reports? They're predicting more snow tonight. Several inches…so Marilyn, the kids, and I aren't going to drive out there tonight. We might go over there tomorrow. Is that all right?"

"Sure, you don't want to take any chance." A frown formed on her weathered face, causing her wrinkles to deepen, wrinkles not often noticed. Now she looked more her age.

"What's wrong, Gramma?" asked Caroline.

She reached deep inside to smile and sound cheery. "That'll be fine, Bob. Have you talked to your brother and sister?"

"No, Marilyn and I just decided now ourselves. I'll call them and have them call you. If you need anything, just call, and I'll venture out myself."

"Don't worry, Bob. We'll be all right. Tell Marilyn and the kids Merry Christmas."

"I will." The phone clicked.

"What did Uncle Bob want, Gramma?" questioned Caroline.

"He just called to say he and Aunt Marilyn won't be coming over tonight because we might have some more snow. It's probably more Aunt Marilyn than your uncle."

"What about Aunt Marilyn?" asked Josh as he blew on his hands that were red from the cold to get them warm.

"Why didn't you wear your gloves, young man?" scolded his grandmother.

"I wasn't out there that long."

"Your uncle Bob called to say they weren't coming tonight because of all the snow."

"It started snowing a little when I was out there now," reported Josh.

"What about Uncle Lyle and Aunt Nancy?" chimed in Caroline as she watched her grandmother put away the good China they always used for special occasions.

"I don't know. Uncle Bob said he'd call them and have them call me. I don't think they'll come either, especially if it's starting to snow again like Josh said. We'll still get you cleaned up and wait for their calls."

They went into the front living room before going upstairs to look out the front picture window. The snow came down in big, fluffy flakes so big you could see designs in each one.

"Is it true, Gramma, that no snowflake is the same?" inquired Caroline.

"That's what they say, dear."

The flakes gradually became smaller and increased in number, becoming a finer snowfall. "I guess we're going to get another storm after all like they predicted," said Josh, who opened the front door to look outside.

"Shut the door, Josh. I believe you're right."

A bunch of house sparrows and juncos were out front gathering the cornbread crumbs Caroline and Gramma put out for them.

"Well, the birds came over for Christmas Eve, Gramma," Caroline said, touching her nose to the frosted windowpane and her breath freezing on the glass, forming snow crystals.

"They sure did, Caroline. They sure did. Let's get that bath of yours now."

Josh went and sat in front of the flickering orange and blue flames with the embers chasing one another like fireflies. He was sure Uncle Lyle and Aunt Nancy wouldn't be coming either.

With the family not coming over, he wouldn't be able to ask his uncle Bob what to do about the skeleton. A strange premonition came over him. The whistling sounds and other strange noises he heard earlier in the ravine piped up outside. Josh stoked the fire and put on another piece of post oak, trying to warm himself. He felt cold and alone despite standing in front of the blazing fire.

CHAPTER 10

Gramma braided her long pumpkin-and-silver-streaked hair, which she rarely did. As she finished putting on some Christmas carols, the phone rang. Josh went to the front window, and he felt the cold from outside through the old window. The snow began falling again. At first the flakes were so large that Josh saw their designs. Grandpa used to say that no two snowflakes were the same, just like people. He decided that only the three of them would be celebrating Christmas together. He wondered how his grandmother would do this first Christmas without Grandpa and now none of her children.

"That was Uncle Bob again," Gramma said. "No one's coming over tonight but maybe tomorrow if the snow lets up. It's just us. I'll make some hot chocolate for you two and some tea for myself."

Gramma always drank hot tea, winter or summer, with lots of milk of course. That was just her way.

The fire had dwindled since Josh was last standing in front of it. He'd changed into a pair of red-and-black checkered flannel pajamas. He didn't hear the whistling sounds or mysterious noises any longer and was comforted by the feel of the soft flannel against his skin. The softness reminded him of his mother's skin, but that seemed like a long time ago.

"Josh, throw on some bigger pieces of wood on the fire. Let's get it warm and cozy in here tonight."

"Sure, Gramma, how many?" asked the disappointed boy.

"Oh, two good-sized pieces, maybe three. And, Caroline, get some cookies out of the cookie jar. We'll sit in front of the fireplace, and I'll tell you about the first Christmas your grandpa and I spent together in Oregon."

Surprised, Josh said, "I never knew you and Grandpa lived in Oregon." He left the room and came back with the extra firewood.

When Josh returned, Gramma and Caroline were already parked in front of the fireplace. They wrapped themselves in an old quilt that Gramma made years ago, which all the kids loved to snuggle in because it was soft and thick, made from scrap pieces of flannel and velvet. It looked like the multicolored robe of Joseph in the Bible. Gramma also enjoyed reading the story of Joseph and his brothers to them, but tonight the story would be a new story about her and Grandpa's first Christmas together in Oregon.

"Throw those logs on the fire, Josh, and I'll start my story," encouraged Gramma.

"Yeah, hurry up, Josh," chimed in his sister.

Josh ignored Caroline's comment and put the collected wood on the fire. He sat next to Gramma on the other side from Caroline. No quilt for him; he was a man.

"C'mon over, Flash," called Josh, and the dog came over, trying to lick Josh. "Just lie down, boy, and stop all the licking." Flash burrowed in next to Josh's legs. Josh stroked him as the dog wagged his tail from side to side slowly. "Good boy."

"Grandpa and I went up to see an old army buddy of his who was dying. Your grandpa was quite bothered and saddened by the illness of his old army buddy. He told me something on the way up there I never knew until then. His buddy Chet Billings saved your grandpa's life during the war. He didn't tell me how but just that he did."

"You never asked him again later?" asked Josh.

"No, I always respected those things your grandpa preferred to keep to himself." Gramma paused for a minute. The wind howled and blew against the house.

Frozen redbud branches brushed against the windowpanes of the family room they occupied. The fire burned well now, and the yellow-orange flames climbed up the chimney. Embers popped off, falling under the iron grate, and glowed sunburn red. Josh and his sister snuggled closer to their sturdy, rugged grandmother whose hair was once the color of the flames that burned before them. Despite her sternness, a more compassionate woman did not exist in the children's eyes, for she and Grandpa took them in when no one else would. The flames continued to skyrocket up the chimney as the fire threw off more heat as the new logs caught fire.

"I like watching the flames dance and flicker off the logs," mused Josh. "It's like magic."

"I know what you mean, Josh," said Gramma. "It has a beauty all of its own. Your grandpa had a great respect for fire and the smoke that it produced."

"So, what was wrong with Grandpa's friend?" inquired Caroline.

"I never did know, and Grandpa never did say, but his friend Chet did not look well when we arrived. He was thin, pale, and had black circles around his eyes, which were sunken in his head like a skeleton."

Skeleton. Josh's thoughts returned to the skeleton in the truck. *Why did Gramma have to describe Grandpa's friend as a skeleton? Had the skeleton in the truck been sick?*

For most of the day, Josh kept images of the skeleton out of his conscious thoughts. Now the mention of skeleton by Gramma temporarily returned him to this morning's scene, and he heard a whistling outside. Was the ghost lurking outside the old farmhouse in the dark?

"What did Grandpa do when he saw his friend?" Caroline questioned, reaching for another chocolate chip cookie.

"Grandpa didn't say much. He just sat quietly with his buddy. Chet told a few stories, and Grandpa just listened. That was Grandpa's way."

"What kind of stories?" asked Caroline.

"Different ones, mostly about being in the army with their old war buddies and what happened to some of them."

Josh left the thoughts of his own skeleton behind and asked, "Did they talk about the war?"

"No, they never did. Your grandfather would never talk about the war, and it's just as well."

"Did Grandpa's friend have any family?" asked Josh.

"No, he never married. He said he had some war injuries and didn't want a wife to have to care for him. He was in the Veteran's Hospital when we were there."

"That's too bad," said Josh.

"Yes, but he seemed to perk up when he saw Grandpa. Chet seemed to be in better spirits while we were there for those few days."

"What's a veteran's hospital?" questioned Caroline as she slid down to put her head on a pillow.

"It's a hospital where men and women who have fought for our country can receive medical care."

"Sounds like he was a lonely guy," Josh commented, and he took a handful of chocolate cookies.

"Don't take them all," whined his sister.

"Hush, young lady," Gramma scolded Caroline, "there're plenty more." Josh wrinkled his nose up at his sister who returned the favor.

"I see you two, and it's not too late for Santa Claus to skip this place."

"Oh, no," cried Caroline, "he'll stop here, won't he?"

"We'll just have to see," said her grandmother in a sympathetic tone. "Well, anyway, we started back home and got to some place in the mountains of Colorado when it started snowing something awful. I was afraid we were going to have a wreck on those old mountain roads. It got worse and worse, and I finally convinced Grandpa to pull into some cabins.

"Were they nice?" asked Caroline.

"Being newly married, we didn't have much money, but we had no choice. The people that ran the cabins were really nice and felt sorry for us when we told them our story. They invited us to eat with them and their family. They had four small children."

"How old were they, Gramma?" questioned Caroline.

"Oh, I don't know, Caroline. I was just thinking about our own family back home and whether we would get home in time for Christmas. But the snowstorm was about like the one we're having tonight. I thought we would never get out of that place in time to get home for Christmas."

"Did you?" Josh asked.

"Yes, after a few days, it let up. Grandpa helped around the cabins doing some repairs on them, and they only charged us half the cost for staying and eating there. We barely made it home in time for Christmas. I didn't have any presents bought or made, and all the stores were already closed by the time we got in Christmas Eve."

"So, what did you do?" asked Caroline, yawning.

"I made pies, bread, and cookies to give to everyone."

"That would've been good enough for me!" exclaimed Josh.

"Oh, Lordy, I'm sure it would've for you, Josh. Let's say our prayers here and then get to bed before Santa Claus comes here and has to skip over our house."

"Oh, no!" cried Caroline, and she hid under the quilts.

CHAPTER 11

The phone rang, and Josh sprang up to answer it.

"Hi, Josh, how ya' doin'?" asked Bobby, who was older than Josh but in the same grade. Josh's grandmother didn't like Josh hanging around with Bobby.

"Okay…"

"Who is it, Josh?" asked his grandmother.

"It's just Bobby, Gramma."

"Mercy me. It's late, and you need to be in bed," called his irritated grandmother. "What's he calling for anyway at this time of night, on Christmas Eve no less?"

"Oh, I don't know. He probably just wants to talk. I won't take long, Gramma."

"Don't be long, Josh Jones."

He knew his gramma meant business when she called him Josh Jones. "I won't be but a minute."

"Likely story. Well, make it quick, young man. If you ask me, that boy is too wild for his own good."

"He's okay, Gramma." But Josh knew better. Bobby did some crazy things and usually was in trouble at school. Josh thought it was because he had no dad, and he lived with his mom and younger brother. His dad died in the Korean War, and his mother gave all her attention to his brother and spent time trying to find another husband.

"What's goin' on, Josh? Have you been outside today?" asked Bobby.

"Yes, but I can't talk long because my grandmother wants me to get to bed."

"Bed…is she crazy? Who can sleep on Christmas Eve with all this snow?"

"Watch what you say about my grandmother."

"Sorry. I didn't mean it. So, what did ya do today?"

Josh moved around the corner into the hallway to have some privacy. The phone had a long black coiled cord that would let him do that.

"I went for a walk down by the ravine with Flash, and I saw a…" Josh tried to stop himself, but it was too late. At the mention of his name, Flash came over and lay down by his feet.

"What did you see? A what?"

"I didn't say," blurted Josh, kicking at the floor like a bull ready to make his charge.

"What's with you, Josh? You can tell me. I'm your best friend, and I won't tell anyone."

"Yeah, sure, just like the time you told all the guys that my grandmother makes me read to my sister at night before she goes to bed." He hesitated.

"Oh, that's different."

"Why, because you say so?" retorted Josh in frustration at having opened the door to Bobby's harassment. When Bobby wanted to know something, he didn't stop until he found the answer. Too bad he wasn't like that in class. "Besides, I don't know who to tell."

"Tell what?" pressed Bobby.

"I saw a skeleton in a truck down in the ravine."

"You saw a what?"

"A skeleton."

"Are you sure?"

"Sure, I'm sure. I'm not dumb."

"I didn't say you're dumb."

"Well, you asked me if I was sure, it was a skeleton like I didn't know what one looked like."

"Get over it. You think too much."

"Easy for you to say."

"Man, you better not tell anyone. There'll be all kinds of questions. I'll try to get over there tomorrow afternoon, and then you can show me," Bobby said excitedly. Bobby was familiar with these kinds of situations, having had some brushes with the law.

"No. Tomorrow's Christmas," said Josh, upset. He knew Bobby would be all over this one like mosquitoes on a hot summer night down by the pond. "You said you wouldn't tell anyone."

"I'm not. I just want to see it myself."

"I have another problem."

"What's that?" pushed the older boy.

"The truck is on the old Cheyenne campground where my grandparents told me to stay out of, and now I've gone on it."

"So what?" Rules never bothered Bobby. Rules were for other people, not him.

"I've disobeyed them, Bobby."

"Don't worry about it. You can say you saw it from the edge of your own land," suggested the anxious boy.

"No, it's too far in there to see the skeleton, plus the snow."

"You worry too much, Josh. Who cares anyway? This is wild."

"I do. My gramma will kill me if she finds out I was in there."

Josh could hear whistling again outside along with the strange noises. The sounds appeared to be at the back door and trying to come into the house. This rattled Josh, and he said more to Bobby than he should.

"Besides, I had a dream about a crow who warned me about a ghost. I've gone against the premonition of the crow."

"C'mon, Josh, you don't believe all that old Cheyenne stuff. Do you?"

Bobby was almost full Cheyenne and did fancy dancing but didn't follow or believe in the old ways. His dad always wanted Bobby to dance, but his dad never saw him dance. Josh believed that was one reason why Bobby never liked to talk about his dad. Josh wanted to learn to dance also, but Grandpa never encouraged it.

"Well, when I found the pickup, there was a crow in a tree right above the truck just like in the dream."

"Coincidence. Crows are all over."

"Yeah, but I heard and keep hearing whistling sounds and peculiar noises like maybe there's a ghost down there. There was one in my dream also."

"There's no ghost," assured the older boy. "It's just the wind with the northerner blowing in this snowstorm."

"Yeah, maybe. I just don't know. I can hear the whistling and spooky noises outside my house right now."

"I can hear whistling too. It's just the storm."

"What about the weird noises?"

"I don't hear those, but maybe you're freaked out and imagined things."

"Yeah right, but you didn't have the dream and find the skeleton."

"Stop worrying about it."

"I can't—"

"Josh, it's time to get off the phone!" yelled his grandmother from upstairs. "Tell Bobby good-bye."

"Okay, Gramma," replied a relieved Josh.

"I gotta hang up, Bobby, and don't come over here tomorrow," warned Josh.

"What's the matter, Josh?" Bobby taunted. "Are you afraid the ghost is going to get you?"

"No, I'm not. Maybe it'll get you."

"Oh yeah, I'm afraid of an imaginary ghost."

"Shut up. Let's just leave it alone like you said."

"Josh, I told you to get off the phone, and I mean now."

"I am, Gramma."

"I can hear your gramma," said Bobby. "Merry Christmas, Josh."

"Yeah, Merry Christmas."

"We'll see about the ghost of Christmas Present, Tiny Tim."

"Knock it off, Bobby. I warned you not to come over here."

CHAPTER 12

Josh went to bed, but his thoughts were not of dancing sugarplums and fairies or presents that he might find under the Christmas tree tomorrow morning. Instead, thoughts of the abandoned truck with the skeleton plagued him, and he wasn't successful at making them disappear. When he closed his eyes, the ghost image appeared. He tried covering his head with his grandmother's homemade scrap quilt.

The white-gray ghost moved and swerved continuously, making it hard to identify. He thought at times it looked like an old gray-haired man, but he could not be sure. The ghost didn't make any noise. The whistling sounds always seemed present when the ghost appeared. What was the deal?

When covering his head with Gramma's multicolored quilt didn't work, he turned on to his side facing the frosted pane window. Fine white snow filled the sky like a white piece of paper. The wind gusted occasionally, causing the snow to swirl in gushing rivulets. His room was in the front part of the old farmhouse where he could see the lone yellowish streetlight by the driveway in the front yard. The snow appeared eerie in color around the iridescent light. He watched the snow whip around the streetlight, feeling like he had a huge kaleidoscope to look out his window.

Josh jumped out of bed and ran to the window where he saw the outline of an old man's face, trying to mouth some words with great exaggeration. "No!" the startled youth shouted, and it was gone.

"What's going on in there, Josh?" called his gramma.

"Nothing… I just told Flash to stop licking me."

"Well, all right, get some sleep," encouraged his grandmother.

Josh's thoughts gradually moved to Gramma's Christmas story and whether his relatives would show up tomorrow for Christmas Day. He became irritated with himself for telling Bobby about what he saw, and hopefully, his friend wouldn't be able to come over to see the skeleton. Josh wasn't convinced about Bobby's advice not to tell anyone. That just didn't seem right not to tell anyone. What would the family of the skeleton be thinking, especially at Christmastime? Surely, they missed this person and worried about the whereabouts of their family member. Maybe that's why he saw the face of the old man urging him to tell someone so he could pass on to the next life in peace and not having his family wondering where he was.

Josh thought how awful it would be not to know where a family member was, especially at Christmastime. His thoughts turned to his own dad. He hadn't heard from him in several years. Where was he? Back East still?

All kinds of questions about the skeleton and his dad raced through his head. His head began to hurt, and the whistling started up again. A cold chill caused him to shiver even under Gramma's heavy quilt. He felt like a long icicle slid right down the back of his spine.

Frustrated, Josh rolled over to his other side, putting his back to the window, but with his eyes opened, he saw odd shadows dancing on the far wall. The forms reminded him of what he heard the old ghost dances looked like. The old Cheyenne believed the buffalo would return, dead ancestors would come back to life, a day with no more whites would come, and the Redman would rule the new world. He tried closing his eyes and thinking about the possibility of a new .22 rifle waiting for him under the Christmas tree. Questions of the skeleton still lingered in his head. He especially wondered if he would get in trouble for being on the old Cheyenne campground and not heeding the warning of the messenger crow in his dream. *Are there really ghosts? Is the dead skeleton's ghost seeking me out to take me on its journey to the Milky Way?*

Josh felt the need to speak with his grandpa. He could answer all these questions.

I need your help, Grandpa, please!

Josh drifted off to sleep, and somewhere between consciousness and sleep, Josh saw a male cardinal beneath a piñon pine tree, scavenging around on freshly fallen white snow. Caught off guard and dazzled at the sight of the bird's scarlet-red and black feathers contrasted against the white blanket of snow, he gasped until he saw his grandpa coming around the edge of the piñon tree and walking toward him.

"Nahkohe, Nahkohe!"

"Grandpa…"

"Josh, my grandson, you've been carrying a heavy burden all by yourself. There's no need for that, my son."

"I don't know what to do, Grandpa. If you were here, I could seek your advice."

"Well, I'm here now, and so is our friend, the redbird, providing us with a good omen."

"So, what should I do? Whom should I talk to?"

"Your grandmother, Nahkohe, she'll know what to do. Tell her and show her what you have found and seen. She's a wonderful woman and has helped me many times. Remember the Christmas story in Oregon and Colorado. It was her, Grandson, who convinced me to stop on that snowy night so we wouldn't have an accident. Your gramma will know what to do, Josh."

"I'm afraid, Grandpa."

"You'll be fine. You were brave against the wild pigs today. You knew to run for the truck and jump into it for protection. You did well against those old, mean, wild pigs today, and you'll do well about your discovery."

"What about going into the old Cheyenne campground, Grandpa?"

"You meant no disrespect, Nahkohe. It was an accident, and I believe the old crow messenger wanted you to discover the skeleton and bring this business to a close. After all, the dead need to have a proper burial to make their journey to the Milky Way."

"Okay, Grandpa, I was wondering about that. Is there a ghost after me?"

"Don't worry about any ghosts, Nahkohe. Just do what you need to do and what is right."

"All right, Grandpa. I miss you."

"I understand, Nahkohe, but know that I'm always here with you. Now dream some good dreams. Dream about hunting deer and turkey, Nahkohe. Enjoy Christmas morning, and you'll know when the time is right to tell your grandmother. Trust her, Josh, and tell her I love her."

The old wise man started to leave and paused. "Oh, by the way, Nahkohe, watch out for that friend of yours, Bobby. He's a coyote."

"He means no harm, Grandpa."

"Just the same, be wary of him like a snake."

"Okay, Grandpa, and thank you."

His grandfather disappeared behind the snow-laden red cedar tree, and the red bird flew off. A large black crow in a sycamore tree replaced the colorful redbird, but soon the crow faded, and Josh fell into a deeper sleep, wondering if he would find a .22 rifle under the Christmas tree. His grandpa told him to dream about hunting deer and turkey. Josh pictured himself taking aim on a large six-point buck, slowly squeezing the trigger while inhaling as his grandpa taught him to do on their hunting trips.

The .22 was all he really wanted. He knew Gramma couldn't afford a lot of gifts, and Caroline would expect more because she still believed in Santa Claus.

He saw the usual assortment of clothes and books under the tree. Gramma made sure they always stayed interested in reading. She had been a teacher when she and Grandpa were first married, but after Uncle Lyle was born, she stayed home to raise the children.

Josh drifted further into sleep and no longer thought about Christmas gifts, skeletons, or ghosts. He did not hear the whistling sound any longer or peculiar noises. He was especially pleased with what his grandpa said about his going out to the old Cheyenne campground but having to tell his gramma was a whole different story.

CHAPTER 13

"Josh, let's go down and see what Santa brought us."

Josh rolled over, turning away from his excited sister. "Did Gramma say it was okay?"

"She won't care," she said, trying to pull his covers off him. "C'mon, Josh."

"It's too early, Caroline. Go back to bed. Besides, I'm cold. The fire must be about out." Still half asleep, Josh saw a fine, powdery snow falling outside the window he faced. Snow filled the two bottom corners of the window forming swelling waves at their peak.

"Josh..."

"What?"

"Let's go downstairs," pleaded Caroline.

He figured the worst of the storm must be over because he caught a ray of sun glistening off the snow-covered redbud outside his window.

"Give me fifteen more minutes. Okay?"

"Okay, but only fifteen." His sister sat down on the floor in the far corner of Josh's room and curled up, pulling the collar of her green flannel bathrobe up over her ears as far it would go.

"What are ya' doin'?" asked Josh angrily.

"Waitin' for you."

"Go to your own room."

"Josh…"

"If you want me to get up in fifteen minutes, you better go to your own room." Josh was almost sitting up now, leaning on his side, facing his insistent sister.

"All right," his sister said, storming down the hallway to her room.

Quiet again, thought Josh, but he knew his sister would be back in less that fifteen minutes. His brain began to come alive, and he remembered the red cardinal on the snow and the visit with his grandpa in his dream.

Josh slumped down and dozed back off to sleep.

"Fifteen minutes is up, Josh, and you said—"

"I know what I said. Are you sure that was fifteen minutes?"

"I'm sure."

"All right. It's no use," Josh conceded. "We'll go downstairs. You probably got coal in your stocking for how you're acting anyway."

"No, I didn't. I've been good," she cried excitedly. "I've helped Gramma around the house a lot."

"Sure, you did." He fumbled to put on his homemade blue flannel robe. Caroline had on her red flannel pajamas with green, yellow, and blue lollipops all over them. "Did you and Gramma leave out cookies for Santa?"

"Yes, whaddya think?"

When Caroline saw Josh put on his bathrobe, she swung around and ran right into Flash who was already standing at the door waiting for them. Startled, Flash jumped and knocked her back into the room where she landed on the floor.

Josh started laughing.

"It's not funny."

"Sure it is."

"Flash shouldn't have been in my way."

"He was there first." Josh covered his mouth to hold back additional laughter.

"Who cares? He's just a dog."

Flash tried to lick Caroline while she sat on the floor. "Stop it, Flash."

"Come here, Flash," called Josh, and with one leap he was on the bed next to Josh.

Caroline was up and brushing off her pajamas. "Are you comin' or not?"

"I'm comin'. Hold your horses."

Caroline disappeared out the door, and Josh heard his sister hopping down the stairs. He was ready to follow her, and then he remembered Grandpa's advice to talk to his grandmother about what he saw in the ravine yesterday. Josh recalled the actual sight of the snow-covered pickup truck and skeleton. A chill went through Josh's whole body. He wondered if the person died immediately or suffered while waiting to be found, not being able to move. *Did the person scream for help, or could they? Did they try to commit suicide? Didn't seem like the best way to do it. How much of the remains did animals eat after the person died?* Then he remembered Bobby's advice not to tell anyone because he wanted to see for himself. He preferred Grandpa's advice, but Bobby was—

"Josh, look what I got..."

Josh was almost to the bottom of the stairs, and he could see his ecstatic, innocent sister holding a handcrafted porcelain doll Gramma's made. His grandmother was very creative in making such things. He wondered if his mother would've been that way also.

"Whaddya think, Josh? Isn't she pretty?"

"Looks just like you," he responded distractedly.

"No, she doesn't. She has black hair, and I have red hair."
"Details, details."

Again, Josh had a flashback of the skeleton and the wild pigs. A whistling sound came from somewhere, but he wasn't able to figure out where it was coming from at the moment. He wasn't even sure if it was just in his own head or coming from outside.

"Look, Josh." His sister grabbed him and tugged on his arm. She pointed to the shiny black metal gun barrel standing in the corner behind the Christmas tree.

"I got it. I got the twenty-two rifle. Wow!"

A cascade of emotions for Josh erupted at that moment. Finding the skeleton on the old Cheyenne campground and what to do about it, fending off the wild pigs, Christmas Eve being different with no big family celebration, the snowstorm, the ghost, and now this, the one thing he wanted for Christmas, was under the tree. Maybe Santa Claus did exist after all, or better yet, maybe he had a pretty great grandmother.

The whistling noise started again, and he saw the ghost outside the frosted front window. He lifted his new .22 rifle and aimed it at the front window. Both the ghost and shrill noise faded.

"Should we get Gramma up?" asked Caroline.

Startled, Josh said, "She's probably getting up right now with the racket you're making."

"Me? What about you? Besides, you're just saying that to make me mad."

"Yeah, right," blurted Josh as he rubbed the cold, smooth barrel of his new rifle.

"You can't make me mad because I got a new doll named Susie."

"Susie? Why Susie?"

"Because I like that name."

"Okay, suit yourself. I thought you might call her Ethel."

"Ethel!" shrieked his sister.

Josh twitched like when biting into a piece of aluminum foil at the sound of his sister's voice.

"Ethel? That sounds like an old person," continued Caroline.

"Old people were once young, Caroline," said Gramma, stepping into the room, pleased to see the happiness in both her grandchildren's eyes over their treasured gifts. Her hair was still in one long braid over her shoulder, exposing more of her auburn hair rather than the silver that was rapidly overtaking the red. She moved slowly with her arthritis acting up because of the cold weather.

It won't be long before she'll need to use a cane, thought Josh. The vision of his grandmother using a cane was hard for him to imagine. His grandmother never seemed old to him, different than his grandfather who always appeared old to him with his reddish-brown cracked skin like the Oklahoma red clay soil when rain hadn't fallen in a long time.

"Josh, get some more wood for the fire, please. I'll start breakfast."

"Okay," said Josh, carefully leaning the .22 against the wall. "Caroline and I have something for you first. Get it, Caroline."

"You better be very careful with that rifle, young man. I don't know why Santa Claus brought you such a thing anyway. Doesn't he have better sense than to give an eleven-year-old a gun?"

"I'm almost twelve, and it's just a twenty-two."

"Here, Gramma," said Caroline as she handed her their gift wrapped in red foil Christmas paper. The ribbon was a wide green one, crossing the square package in the middle.

"This is for me? I wonder what it is." Her fingers carefully opened the package without tearing the paper.

"Open it, Gramma. I want to see what it looks like on you."

"Hush, Caroline," said her brother. "Don't tell her what it is."

"I didn't."

"You're about to."

Gramma opened the gift and saw a large straw shade hat with a red ribbon around the brim, which passed through two holes on each side so you could tie it.

"Red's my favorite color."

"We know."

"I've needed a new hat to work outside in the yard and garden. It's beautiful. Let me give you two a hug." She stood up and stepped toward Josh, who tried to get away, but his spry grandmother grabbed him first before he was able to move. He thought he saw tears in her eyes.

"Gotcha," said Gramma, "and Merry Christmas, Josh."

"Merry Christmas, Gramma."

"Me, too," said Caroline, hugging them both.

"I'll get that wood now," he said, as he moved toward the kitchen.

"Remember what I said about that rifle, young man."

"I'll remember," said Josh. He knew he better heed the warning, or he would lose possession of it quicker than the wild pigs came at him yesterday.

Bouncing like a flat stone skipping across a pond, Josh went out the back door after the firewood. The cold air hit him in the face with the force of a professional boxer. A powdery snow similar to the shifted flour his grandmother made when baking still fell. The blast of cold air made him cough and reminded him of his dilemma. *Whom should I tell, if anyone?* A male cardinal started chirping as he flew to the peak of the roof where the firewood was stored. Josh looked up to see the red bird just before it flew off into the early morning sky after scraping his red and yellow beak on the corner of the snow-covered roof. At the same time, a much bigger bird and not as pretty appeared making a big racket. The large crow sat in the post oak next to the lean-to, and Josh knew what he had to do.

CHAPTER 14

Josh kicked his boots against the top step, knocking off the loose snow before he went into the house. Cradling three pieces of cottonwood, Josh struggled to open the screen door, which always stuck when moisture was in the air. He hoped that Gramma wasn't in the kitchen, but as luck would have it, she was putting the finishing touches on the pancakes. Josh liked his pancakes golden brown like a palomino horse that he saw in a July Fourth parade once.

"You ready to eat, Josh?" asked his gramma as she flipped pancakes onto an old Jane Ray white platter trimmed in gold.

"Sure. Let me set these by the fireplace."

"Put two of them on the fire right away and wash your hands. Tell Caroline to come in here to help me set the table."

"Okay."

"Make sure you both wash your hands!" she called to the hurrying boy as he rounded the corner.

When Josh returned to the kitchen, Caroline was already sitting at the table with her new Christmas doll placed in a chair beside her.

"What in the world is your doll doing at the table?" blurted Josh.

"Eating with us."

"No, she ain't," retorted her indignant brother.

"Isn't," said Josh's grandmother.

"Okay, isn't," said Josh.

"Susie isn't a doll," his feisty sister fired back.

"She sure is," taunted the ornery boy. "Can she talk?"

"You both stop it right now," scolded the firm matron, "or I'll take both your favorite present away."

"He started it," cried Caroline.

"Caroline!"

"All right," complained the obstinate girl, but she reluctantly complied, knowing that her grandmother did not make idle threats. She would take Susie away.

"Sit down, Josh. I know that you're hungry."

"I sure am," said her grandson as he pulled the green vinyl and silver chair out from the table.

"You're always hungry," said Gramma as she took her green-and-white apron off, placing it on the coat rack and picking up the platter of piping-hot pancakes.

She sat down and brushed her hair back from her face, exposing a pale forehead with several creases, running across it like a shattered window, and a few remaining brown freckles from long ago.

"Ready to eat?" she asked.

Both children said yes.

"We need to say grace first. After all, it's Christmas Day. The baby Jesus was born. Better yet, Josh, get the Bible, and we'll read about the first Christmas."

"Do I have to?"

"Yes, and quickly because I don't want everything to get cold."

Josh went into the living room, and Flash followed, wagging his bushy black tail from side to side like an American flag in a July Fourth parade in windy Oklahoma. The fire put off a good glow, and Josh was tempted to stay, but he quickly picked up the Bible off the homemade wooden coffee table made from cedar wood that his grandpa-built years ago before he was born. When he stepped into the kitchen, he moved toward his grandmother and attempted to give the well-worn black leather Bible to her, but she told him to read it.

"Turn to Luke chapter two and read verses one through twenty. That will be our grace and church for this snowy, wintry Christmas Day breakfast."

The reluctant boy read the passage, and Gramma responded, "Amen. You did a great job reading, Josh."

"Thanks," the embarrassed boy said, lowering his head.

"Yeah, good job, Josh," chimed in his sister, fixing her new porcelain doll's position at the table.

Josh's head snapped up like a deer with the breaking of a nearby branch, but Gramma intervened before Josh unloaded on his sister.

"Pass me your dish, Josh, and I'll give you some of my best pancakes."

"Sure. Pile them on, Gramma."

"Three's enough for now. Caroline, hand me your plate."

"Okay, Gramma, and I'll give you Susie's too."

Josh lost it. "Susie's?"

"Yeah, Susie's…"

"She's a doll."

"So—"

"You both hush," interrupted Gramma. "She'll have to do with make-believe pancakes."

"Oh…" whined Caroline.

"Caroline."

"Okay, Gramma."

"These are terrific, Gramma," added Josh as he passed his plate for more.

"When you're done eating, Josh, I want you to check the chickens. Make sure the lights are on to help keep the coup warm."

"Can I go with him?" asked Caroline.

"No, I want you to go upstairs and change, and then you can help me do the dishes."

"Why do I have to always help with the dishes and not get to do any outside chores?" Caroline complained.

"Because you're too little and a—"

"Josh," Gramma stopped him before he could say another word.

Caroline wrinkled her nose at him, but he knew enough to stop while he was ahead. Meanwhile, his pouting sister took her doll and went upstairs. Josh continued to poke at his remaining pancakes and stirred the leftover maple syrup on his plate with his fork. Now was as good a time as any to tell his grandmother about the skeleton. Josh forced himself to look at his grandmother sitting directly across from him.

"I saw a skeleton in the ravine yesterday up by the old county road where it curves and drops off. I know you don't like me going that far, but Flash took off running, and I just followed him." At the mention of his name, the family pet wagged his tail from side to side.

"Are you sure?"

"I'm pretty sure. I didn't get very close. I didn't know what to do. I had a dream last night, and Grandpa told me to tell you. He said you'd know what to do."

"Well, there's only one thing to do, and that's tell Sheriff Daniels. We've got to report it. When did you see this?"

"Yesterday morning…early before Caroline or you were up."

"Have you told anyone else?"

"No, uh, yes…"

"Which is it, Josh?"

"I told Bobby Willis last night."

"Why?"

"I just did. I didn't know what to do, and I couldn't get it out of my head."

"There's another one of those I didn't mean to. Well, I'm calling Sheriff Daniels right now."

"Do you think he'll be mad with me?"

"No, Josh, he'll be glad to know. He'll need to start investigating right away. He probably won't like spending Christmas checking out the situation, but that's not your fault. That's what he's paid to do. He'll have to inform and work with the Cheyenne, being on their old tribal lands."

She called Sheriff Daniels, and he said he would try to come over in the afternoon. If he couldn't make it by car, he would ride his horse, and that would take longer.

"Gramma, Grandpa told me to tell you that he loved you."

His grandmother turned away but not before he saw tears in her eyes.

CHAPTER 15

Later that afternoon a heavy knock on the front door woke Josh from his dream about shooting his new .22 rifle in the ravine. Flash's ears perked up and moved to the door even before the knock came. Josh followed slowly, thinking about the huge man he knew was on the other side.

Sheriff Daniels, a big burly man, stood before Josh like the local water tower on the hill above town. He stood six-foot-five and tipped the scale at 275 pounds with a head of brown hair that always looked like a tornado just passed. The town barber rarely saw the sheriff in his chair, and waves of the brown hair curled up at his jacket collar. His eyebrows matched his hair, the former as unruly as the latter and almost touching in the middle over his Santa Claus–type nose. The eyebrows curled and rambled down over his eyelids, threatening to cover his seawater-green eyes. His eyes seemed to sparkle like seawater when the sun hit it at midday.

To look at the giant of a man scared Josh, but once the sheriff spoke, he relaxed. The sheriff always spoke softly like he was telling a secret only meant for your ears. The voice was comforting at the same time, although you knew that he was in charge of any situation. No matter what, you could not help but like this man. The smallest, senseless thing would make him laugh, and when he did, he shook all over like a buckboard going down an old country road. Many referred to him as the "Jolly Green Giant." Behind his back, of course, but the good-natured sheriff knew about the name and used it to his advantage, especially with the young people of the county.

Josh witnessed Sheriff Daniels being stern on a few occasions in the past. The local lawman quickly took control of any rowdy situations or ruffians seeking trouble. Few were foolhardy enough to challenge him, and if they were, they soon regretted it.

One time at the county fair, Sheriff Daniels caught some older guys already out of high school, some graduated and some dropouts, drinking behind the grandstand. Josh was on his way to the horse barn with his grandpa to look at some horses to buy when it all happened. The local wise guys started mouthing off, fueled by the beer they'd been drinking. Without any fanfare, the usual Jolly Green Giant lifted two of them up by their Levi jean jackets to his eye level, which was a considerable height. All four stood frozen and dumbstruck. Their farmers' tans turned ghostly white as the newly fallen snow on the ground outside right now.

Standing like a fortress in the doorway, looming as large as an airplane hangar, Sheriff Daniels wasn't laughing today and had a serious look on his face. The smoke- gray air vapors coming from his huge nostrils made him even more imposing. Josh stepped out of the way to let the sheriff in and looked past the large man, which wasn't an easy thing to do, to see if the sheriff drove his old Willy's Jeep Wagon or rode his horse. The wide-eyed boy saw the sheriff's buckskin mare that had moisture spewing out of her nostrils also. Meanwhile, Sheriff Daniels blew on his massive red, chapped hands trying to warm them. Anxiously, Josh turned toward the "Jolly Green Giant" after closing the door to greet him, but the sheriff spoke first.

"So, Josh, you've got something to show me?"

"Yeah," Josh responded hesitantly.

"Well, what about this dead body?"

"It's not a dead body. It's a skeleton. I saw it yesterday."

Josh's grandmother entered the room with a warm smile.

"Good to see you, Sheriff Daniels. How's your family?"

"Just fine, Mrs. Smith. Thanks for asking."

"Sorry to call you away from them on Christmas."

"It's part of the job, ma'am."

"Still just the same, it seems such a shame. Do you want a cup of coffee, Sheriff?

"Sure do. Could use something to take the chill out of my bones."

"C'mon into the kitchen. Josh, take Sheriff Daniels's coat and hat."

Great, thought Josh. *She's inviting him in like this is a social visit. I just wanna get this over with.* But he complied with his grandmother's wishes.

"So, Sheriff, how's the weather out there?" she asked while pouring him some steaming hot coffee into a Jadeite restaurant-style cup.

The sheriff pulled out the closest kitchen chair to him before answering and sat down. "It's finally slowing down a bit. I don't think we'll get any more snow today, Mrs. Smith."

"Thank goodness. Maybe my family can finally get a chance to come by tomorrow."

"Maybe they can," responded the sheriff picking up the cup of hot coffee with his ruddy, massive hands and gently placing it to his numb lips. He blew on the coffee carefully and took a small sip before placing it back on the table.

"What's taking you so long?" she called to her grandson.

"He's probably trying to prolong our visit to the dead body," offered the sheriff as he took another sip of coffee.

"It's a skeleton," repeated Josh as he stepped into the room as Sheriff Daniels turned to look at him.

"What's this your grandmother tells me about a skeleton in a truck?

"Yes, sir, there down in the ravine."

"Have a seat, son," Sheriff Daniels invited the young boy while pushing a chair out next to himself for Josh.

"Well, how far away is it from here, Josh?"

"Almost to the old road that goes to town down by the Branson's."

The sheriff thought for a minute. "Well, that makes sense. Maybe the person driving fell asleep, drove off the side of the road, lost control, and plunged down into the ravine."

Finally, he's starting to believe me, thought Josh.

"That's a narrow road at the bend in the road without much of a shoulder, and it drops off pretty quickly. You wouldn't see a vehicle down there from the road."

"Yes, sir, that's what I thought," mumbled Josh.

A small patch of silver could be seen along the sheriff's temples as he thought for a moment and then set his cup on the table. "How come you haven't seen it until now if it is a skeleton?"

"Well, I—"

"Sheriff Daniels, you know that my husband, Josh's grandpa, passed away this past Thanksgiving?"

"Yes, ma'am, I did."

"Well, Josh hasn't gone out much since then, and before then, we were up at the hospital all the time."

"I understand. I'm sorry, but I had to ask," apologized the burly man, squirming in his seat.

"I know," responded Josh's grandmother. "No offense taken."

Sheriff Daniels turned to Josh. "You ready to show me where this truck is, Josh?"

"Yes, sir, I'll grab my coat and hat."

"You better put on some mittens too. It's mighty cold out there."

"Yes, sir, I've got some gloves." *Mittens*, thought Josh. *What, does he think I'm a little kid?* Josh, Flash, and Sheriff Daniels went out the back door and headed toward the ravine.

CHAPTER 16

"Lead the way, Josh."

Sheriff Daniels put his massive hand on Josh's shoulder, which felt like the weight of the world, and the tightness in his chest reminded him of a bad chest cold.

Flash charged off in front of them, sometimes disappearing in the high snowdrifts that filled the landscape between the trio and the infamous ravine. The unlikely pair, big and small, covered the ground slowly, stepping through the deep snow, and did not speak for a while until the affable sheriff stopped and said, "Tough going with all this snow and drifts, huh, Josh?"

"Yes, sir, it is. The wind doesn't make it any easier." He pulled his sheepskin collar up around his neck. Cold, Josh wished he'd brought his old wool scarf knitted for him by his grandmother. The twosome paused for a moment for Sheriff Daniels to catch his breath. Flash returned covered with snow, looking like an Oreo cookie. He barked at the both of them as if to say, "Hurry up."

The threesome started their journey again, attempting to skirt the bigger drifts when possible. Flash plowed through the white waves of snow. The dog disappeared time and again like a drowning child in the ocean with his black-and-white streamlined body popping up from time to time.

As they trudged along, Josh heard the big man inhale and exhale in quick gasps with occasional deep, extended breathing. Josh felt sorry for the mountain of a man laboring so hard on Christmas Day and wondered what the sheriff was thinking. He soon found the answer.

"How come you waited until now to tell your grandmother, Josh?"

"I was afraid. I didn't know what to do," answered Josh, agitated that the sheriff was asking him this question again without his grandmother around to help him. *What difference did it make anyway? We're on our way down there now.* That's all that mattered to Josh. He'd have it off his conscience, maybe learn what happened and who it was.

"What were you afraid of?" asked the sheriff, stopping to catch his breath. They were close to the hidden pickup. Flash continued to run ahead, returning and barking his impatience with them both. As they moved closer to the ravine, Flash stayed gone longer.

"Of getting in trouble…I don't know. I was confused. Flash, Flash, come here." Annoyed, the skittish youth continued, "Besides, I'm not supposed to go on the old Cheyenne campground. I thought I would get in trouble for that."

Sheriff Daniels coughed and checked out the surrounding snow-covered area. "Well, let's get movin', Josh, we're burning daylight."

"Sure," responded Josh, although he wasn't in any big hurry to reach the location of the skeleton.

The snow wasn't as deep, and the drifts were less as they moved closer to the ravine. The unlikely pair descended into the ravine. As they did Sheriff Daniels lost his footing and almost fell. Josh almost laughed but caught himself.

"You know, Josh, I'm just doing my job asking these questions?"

"Yeah, I know. The whole thing is just eerie. I can't get it out of my head."

"Yeah, death can be scary, especially when you're not expecting it."

Flash took off again and didn't return. Josh knew they were close. When they approached the red-and-white belly of the ravine, he saw Flash prancing in a circle, and then his chocolate-colored eyes zeroed in on the top of the blue truck. Last night's new- fallen snow nearly covered the abandoned pickup.

The snow they walked on was wetter than when it first began to fall. This type of snow was better for packing snowballs.

"This wet snow is harder to walk through, Josh."

"Yes, sir."

"What's Flash doing? Are we almost there?"

"Just about."

Josh saw Sheriff Daniels leaning forward and squinting in an effort to catch an early glimpse of the deserted truck. The top of the cab was barely visible and the skeleton not at all. As they closed in on the entombed skeleton, Josh noted that the wild pig tracks and their presence were all concealed. They still weren't able to see the mysterious skeleton, and that was okay with Josh.

Attempting to lessen the tension, the Jolly Green Giant asked, "Are you cold yet?"

"You bet I am. This wind is a killer. It cuts like a wild hog's teeth."

"That's for sure," grunted the winded lawman.

"The ravine helps some."

"Thank God for small miracles."

They trudged forward. The wind continued to sway the heavy, snow-laden branches with the rhythm of a porch swing in the summer. Sometimes platters of snow fell off, making poof sounds. Thrown in the mix were swoosh noises when the wind kicked up, leaving Josh to think about if the skeleton's ghost was still seeking a body not having been buried yet. The mood was eerie and different than yesterday.

"Josh," the sheriff startled him, "why did you decide to tell your grandmother?"

Here he goes again with the questions.

"I don't know," Josh said as he looked away from his inquisitor. "I just did. It seemed like the right thing to do."

"Why's that?" asked Sheriff Daniels as he moved closer to the truck in question with the alleged skeleton in it. Flash sniffed around the snow-covered pickup, focusing on the side where the wild pigs launched their attack.

The sheriff began circling the old truck, keeping about a five-foot distance from the mystery vehicle. On the driver's side, the sheriff took off one of his cowhide gloves and used it to clear snow away until he felt and then saw the long bone of the skeleton's forearm dangling outside the broken window.

"Well, Josh, you were right. It's a skeleton all right."

No foolin' Sherlock.

"You never did answer my question about why you thought it was the right thing to do, telling your grandmother."

When is he going to give it a rest? He played along and said, "I just did. It took me some time to decide, but I thought someone might be worrying about a family member and looking for them."

"You have a point there, Josh."

"Yeah, I would want to know if I were them, especially being Christmas and all."

"That's true."

Once again Sheriff Daniels's questions aggravated him. He kind of wished he hadn't told his grandmother after all. *Let someone else find the body and deal with the dead person's ghost. Well, it's too late now. What's done is done.* That's what his grandmother always told him. Besides, his grandpa was the one who told him to tell his gramma, and that was what he did. And his grandpa was always right.

Sheriff Daniels kept moving slowly around the truck, still maintaining a good distance from it and looking intently.

"Looks like some large animals have been here recently. The bark on the trees is scuffed up like something has been rubbing against them."

The snow from last night covered the wild pig tracks, but Josh hadn't noticed the abraded trees like the sheriff did.

"Yeah, right before Flash and I got ready to leave, some wild pigs charged us. I slipped climbing up the side of the ravine but was able to make it into the bed of the pickup."

"Lucky you. Did you tell your grandmother about that?"

"No, sir."

"Probably a good thing," said the sheriff with a trace of a smile forming under his large bushy moustache. "The wild pigs would've been easier on you than your grandmother."

"That's true enough, sir, but it didn't seem so at the time."

"I imagine." The bulky man chuckled. "You can head home, Josh. I'm about done here for now."

"Sounds great to me, Sheriff."

"It's getting late, and with all this snow, I won't be able to tell much anyway. Hopefully the weather will be better tomorrow. When I come back, I'll bring some more people to help dig out the snow. Besides, I need to inform the Cheyenne that it's on their old campground."

"C'mon, Flash, let's head for home."

At first, the dog was hesitant but finally chased after Josh as he started back. Josh tried to step in the footprints made on the way down while going up the ravine. He especially tried to step in Sheriff Daniels's footprints because they were much bigger and deeper. Josh couldn't hit each one of the sheriff's because they were farther apart than his own.

"Josh," called the sheriff, "if I need anything else or need to ask you any more questions, I'll call you or your grandmother. Be careful on the way back."

Great, thought Josh, *how many more questions can he ask me?* "Can you believe that Flash?"

Flash stayed by Josh's side this time until they climbed out of the ravine. At the top of the climb, the northerner smacked him hard right in the face, like the barn doors slamming shut when a good gust of wind came along. That's when he heard the familiar whistling sound from yesterday.

"Do you hear that, Flash? Is that ghost still here?"

Flash stood still with his ears straight up as if he saw the ghost but quickly gave up and barked at Josh as they continued to move.

Josh patted the spotted dog on the head. After they covered some ground, Josh asked Flash another question, "Why did Sheriff Daniels keep asking me all those questions? You'd think he thought I caused the truck to drive off the road."

Flash barked as if to agree and ran ahead of the tired boy. *The sheriff is right, thought Josh. It is getting late, and it won't be long before it is dark.* Josh was cold and ready to get into a warm house. It had been a long two days, and he was glad they were soon to be finished.

As the twosome approached the house, the faint appearance of a half-moon began to show itself in the northern sky. A few of the larger stars were also noticeable. Josh could see whitish-gray smoke billowing out of the stone chimney on the side of the old farmhouse and yellowish light in the bottom floor windows. The snow was almost to the windowsills of the first-floor wood-framed windows. The scene looked like a Currier and Ives Christmas card that his grandmother enjoyed receiving. He was glad to be almost home. Flash ran circles around the weary boy and nipped at his heels.

"I hope Gramma has some hot chocolate made. That sure would taste and feel great."

Josh smelled something cooking that made him hungrier than he already was. *Did Gramma cook the turkey anyway, even though no one came over for Christmas.*

Flash resumed running, and Josh attempted to run the remaining four hundred yards to the inviting farmhouse in front of him. The anticipation of warmth and Gramma's home cooking jump-started his enthusiasm for about two hundred yards. He slowed, and Flash chased back to him. The dog leaped up on the bent-over boy and playfully knocked him to the ground. Josh laughed, and it felt like old times before all this happened.

"Take it easy, Flash."

Flash barked and nudged at the boy.

"I'm going as fast as these stumpy legs will carry me."

They finally arrived at the back doorsteps, and Josh stomped the snow off his boots. He climbed the few rickety wooden steps and opened the back door. When he stepped in, he saw Gramma sitting at the old green vinyl and chrome kitchen table set with her head down, crying.

"What's wrong, Gramma? Is everything okay?"

His grandmother sat up quickly, wiping tears from her weathered face, and smoothed back her silver-streaked, pumpkin-colored hair.

"Yes, Nahkohe, I was thinking about Grandpa and got to missing him. Did you show Sheriff Daniels the location of the truck?"

"Yes. He told me to go home, and he will be in touch if he needs anything else." Josh moved over to his grandmother and put his arms around her from behind, and she patted his hands.

"Josh, your hands are cold. Go warm them up by the fire. Do you want some hot chocolate? I've got some made."

"Sure. It sounds great. It's awfully cold out there. Did you make turkey and stuffing?" Josh loved his gramma's stuffing.

"Why, of course, Nahkohe. Warm your hands, which looked just like your grandpa's Cheyenne hands for a few minutes. Then get your sister, and we'll have our own Christmas dinner."

"Okay, Gramma."

Josh went into the living room where the stone fireplace was and stood in front of it with his red, chapped hands extended over the burning cedar logs. He savored the sweet smell of the red-streaked wood. His grandmother rarely used his Cheyenne name. She respected the special bond he and his granddad had between them, but her thinking about Grandpa must have brought back all those little things that reminded her of him. Josh knew that he reminded her so much of his grandpa.

The warm house felt good, and the absence of the whistling and spooky noises wasn't a bad deal either. Josh felt a sense of being the man of the house. A big burden was lifted from his small shoulders, but they felt bigger for the moment.

CHAPTER 17

Josh warmed his hands at the fireplace and then went upstairs to tell his sister it was time to eat.

"It's turkey time, Turkey," teased Josh.

"Quit it, Josh, or I'll tell Gramma."

"Yeah, like I'm scared."

"Gram—"

"Okay, okay. I'm sorry."

"That's better," said his sister, pleased with herself for winning that small victory. "What did you show Sheriff Daniels?"

"Something I found yesterday morning in the ravine."

"I know that, but what was it?"

Josh ignored the question as they ran down the stairs. Caroline poked her brother and asked, "C'mon, Josh, what did you show him?"

"You're too nosey, Caroline."

"No, I'm not."

"No, you're not what?" asked Gramma as they made their way into the kitchen, filled with all the aromas of Gramma's cooking.

Josh loved the smell of French apple pie cooking with the aromas of apples, cinnamon, and raisins fusing together. His grandmother's kitchen always seemed filled with homemade cooking scents.

"Sit down, you two, and stop fussing."

"I'm not fussing, Gramma. Caroline keeps bugging me about what I showed Sheriff Daniels."

"Caroline, stop pestering your brother. You have no need to know about that. It's between Josh and Sheriff Daniels."

Gramma put the golden-brown turkey with touches of black in the middle of the table.

"How's that look?"

"Great, and it smells awesome, Gramma. It looks like your best ever."

"You're just saying that Josh, because you'd eat anything right now."

"No, you're just the best cook I know.'

"Oh, hush, Nahkohe."

Josh stole a look at his grandmother because once again she called him Nahkohe.

"Let's say grace and give thanks, you two. Bow your heads."

Gramma said grace, and Josh thought he heard the pious lady's voice crack and waver just a bit as she finished saying the prayer of thanks. Christmas had been tough on her without Grandpa, her sons, and their families not being able to be there either. Josh knew that she was a strong lady and gained much from her faith.

"Gramma, I want white meat with some gravy and cranberry sauce," said Caroline as she passed her white China plate trimmed in a fine gold line on the edge of the plate where the plate formed its lip.

Josh helped himself to some sweet potatoes, green beans with bacon, and some of Gramma's piping hot homemade rolls waiting his turn for the turkey.

"Where's Susie?" asked Josh. "She's not eating with us tonight?"

"No, she's in bed, silly."

"I'm silly? Isn't it passed—"

"Josh, that's enough. What kind of turkey do you want?" asked his grandmother.

"Some of both, please, and lots of dressing."

"Well, there's plenty. Oh, by the way, Bobby called after you and Sheriff Daniels left. Why does he keep calling you? What does he want?"

"He probably wants to know about the skeleton."

"Skeleton!" shrieked Caroline. "What skeleton?"

"The one I found in the ravine yesterday. Sorry, Gramma, it just slipped out."

"It's okay, Josh. She'd probably find out sooner or later."

"So, what about the skeleton, Josh? You saw a skeleton?"

"Yes," said Josh with a sigh.

"Where?"

"In an old, abandoned pickup truck down in the deepest part of the ravine on the old Cheyenne campground."

"I thought you weren't supposed to go there."

"I'm not, but I lost track of where I was with all the snow and Flash running all over the place going crazy."

"Were you scared?"

"No, why would I be?"

"I don't know. It sounds creepy to me."

"That's why we didn't tell you in the first place."

"That's enough about the skeleton," said Gramma. "You can call Bobby later and tell him Sheriff Daniels is taking care of it now."

Reluctantly, Josh responded, "Okay." He knew Bobby would chide him for telling his grandmother and the sheriff before the older boy could see the skeleton.

"Josh, when you finish eating, get some more wood for the fireplace. It's supposed to be cold again tonight."

"Sure, Gramma. This is the best turkey you ever cooked."

"It's pretty darn good if I don't say so myself," said Gramma with a faint smile on her lips.

"Did you make any pies, Gramma?" asked Josh.

"Now what do you think?"

"What kind?"

"Pumpkin, cherry, and French apple."

"Too many to pick from," expressed Josh.

"I know which one I'll have," said Caroline.

"Which one?" inquired Gramma.

"Pumpkin with whipped cream."

"And that's what you'll have, young lady," said Grandmother as she turned to look at the pies cooling in the cabinet. "Have you decided which one you'll have, Josh?"

"It's tough, but I'll have French apple."

Gramma pushed her chair from the table and went to the counter. The gray-haired matron opened the old wooden pie cabinet and took the pies out. The sweet aroma of freshly baked homemade pies flooded the room with their enticing smells. Josh could already taste the apple-cinnamon-raisin and flaky homemade crust.

"I can taste the French apple pie already, Gramma."

Gramma cut healthy pieces for each of her grandchildren. She ambled back over to the table, carrying both plates.

"Pumpkin with whipped cream for you young lady and French apple for you."

Caroline took the pie with whipped cream on top of it looking like the snowy landscape outside their window and relished its appearance. Caroline savored its aroma for a few seconds and then turned to her grandmother and proclaimed with an air of reverence, "You're a great grandmother, and I miss Grandpa."

"I know, dear. I do too."

Josh finished his French apple pie, pushed his stuffed body away from the table, and announced, "Well, I'm full, and it sure was good. I'll get the wood now."

"Thank you and take a look at the chickens. See if they need any more feed."

"Okay."

"Can I help?" chimed in Caroline.

"No, you can help me with the dishes and cleaning up this messy kitchen."

"Ah…"

"Be careful, little lady."

"Okay, Gramma."

"That's a relief," Josh told Flash as they stepped outside and the cold air assaulted them, as if they stepped into an old icehouse. "I'll check the chickens first. You stay here." Flash barked his protest but complied. When he came back, he saw a crow, much to his unnerving, sitting on the telephone line leading to the silhouetted house. He noticed the big black bird holding something in its black beak. He couldn't tell what it was.

"Why is the messenger still here?" Josh wondered aloud to Flash, almost dropping his load of wood for the fireplace. Josh knew that his grandmother would be pleased with him for gathering the wood without her having to tell him. The sheriff knew about the skeleton now, and the case rested in his capable hands. What was left to be done? One thing that pleased him was that he didn't hear the whistling and noises any longer. *Is the skeleton's ghost happy now?*

"Let's get inside the house, Flash. It feels creepy out here tonight."

Flash barked and ran to the back door ahead of Josh and scratched on it.

As Josh moved to follow the dog's lead, the black crow messenger swooped down, almost hitting him as he started to run. Josh ducked, coming close to falling, but he caught his balance as the bird flew over him and continued past the rooftop.

"What the heck?" Josh saw a green cedar branch that the diving crow dropped in front of him. With his adrenaline pumping, Josh picked up the single bough and puzzled over it. *Is this a peace offering?* mused the anxious boy.

As the dog scratched at the back door, Caroline opened it. Josh quickly threw the cedar branch aside and stepped inside the toasty-warm house.

"What's wrong?" asked his sister. "You look frightened."

"Nothing."

"Well, great, and good timing because Gramma and I just finished cleaning the kitchen and doing the dishes. You wanna play a game with me, Josh?"

"Not right now. I'm going to call Bobby."

"Okay, after?"

"Maybe if it's not too late."

CHAPTER 18

Josh called Bobby later that night and told him all that happened with Sheriff Daniels. He expressed his frustration with the sheriff, asking him so many questions and acting like he had something to do with it.

"I told you not to tell anyone," said his friend on the other end of the line. "Why did you tell them before I got to see the skeleton? Now it will be gone before I see it for myself."

"I had to tell them. I couldn't get the skeleton out of my head. It was bugging the heck out of me, and besides, that's what my grandpa said to do."

"Your grandpa's dead."

"I know, but he visited me in a dream."

"In a dream?" shouted Bobby.

"Yes."

"Get real, Josh," chided the older boy. "You're dreamin' all right. Did you tell any of the other boys?"

"No, just you, and I'm sorry I told you."

"Why's that?"

"Because you're making fun of me," fought back Josh.

"No, I'm not. I just wanted to see the skeleton for myself. It's not every day you get to see a skeleton in the woods like that. How'd ya feel when you saw it?"

"Weird, almost creepy until the wild hogs came."

"Wild hogs? You didn't tell me about them. What happened?"

Now Josh felt like he had something on Bobby.

"When I was leaving, I fell going up the side of the ravine and hurt my ankle. That's when they came charging after me."

"Whaddya do?"

"I was able to make it into the back of the pickup before they got to me."

"The one with the skeleton?"

"Yes, it wasn't a parking lot."

Josh took great delight in giving back to Bobby some of his own medicine for a change.

"Wow."

"It's funny now, but it wasn't then."

"Josh, it's time to get off the phone," called his grandmother, but Josh was having too good of a time messing with and having something over Bobby, but he reluctantly complied.

"Okay, Gramma," responded Josh. "I gotta get off the phone, Bobby. I'll talk to you later."

"Yeah, sorry you thought I was mad with ya'."

"It's okay. It's over now I hope."

"You'll have to finish your story about the wild hogs."

"Sure. Talk to you later."

Josh hung up and felt good about having the wild hog story to lord over his friend, Bobby.

"Josh, you ready to play a game now?" Asked Caroline.

"No, I think I'll get some more wood for the fire".

'You just brought some in."

"It wasn't enough."

Josh looked out the front room door. The night sky was clear and stygian black except for the crescent moon and a few stars. *Maybe life will get back to normal*, thought Josh. He could only hope.

Josh turned around and walked to the back door, pulled his jacket off the coat hook in the pantry, and stepped outside into the frigid night. He took a deep breath and blew it out, watching the white vapor hang in the air and then slowly float off up into the sky. Flash nudged him, and Josh stooped down and petted his faithful companion who wagged his tail faster. He kicked the drifted snow between the house and lean-to as he moved toward the three-sided homemade building covered with snow, looking almost like a snowdrift itself. Once he made it to the front, he bent over to pick up some firewood. A raccoon scurried from behind the trashcans along the other end of the house. Flash lit out after the dark shadow, chasing the masked bandit creature toward the edge of the ravine, and then stopped.

"He got the best of you, buddy," called Josh, but Flash hunkered down motionless. Josh took a chill about the same time Flash began to prowl the edge of the ravine heading toward the direction where they found the truck and skeleton.

"Where ya' goin', Flash?" asked Josh, moving cautiously toward the ravine himself.

"What do you hear?" His dog kept moving stealthily along the ravine, paying no attention to his master. The dog continued as if being drawn by a magnet.

Josh dropped the wood he was carrying and approached the edge of the ravine himself. They both stopped at the same time as if they hit an invisible wall.

"I hear it, Flash, barely, but I hear it."

Tree limbs swayed slightly like something was blowing on them with snow falling to the ground below them.

"Flash, those branches are moving without any wind." His dog didn't stir, and neither did Josh.

Flash's ears perked up like standing at attention for a boot-camp drill instructor and pushed forward in the same direction as the swaying limbs were moving.

"I don't think this is a good idea, Flash." But his intense canine companion didn't stop his pursuit.

"Flash, halt. Now." But his normally obedient friend ignored Josh's command.

"What's with you, Flash?" The dog proceeded farther up the edge of the ravine, and Josh could not see him any longer. He feared following the stalking dog and disobeying his grandmother twice. Josh knew something wasn't quite right with Flash and questioned his own feelings, which were usually accurate, being intuitive by nature. His grandfather always said he had that gift.

Flash disappeared into the black hole of the ravine, and the whistling noises intensified, drawing Josh down into the ravine once again against his better judgment, but the noise was different than before. The sound was more enticing than frightening this time. Josh followed even though he couldn't find Flash at the moment.

"Flash, Flash, where are you?" With his next step, Josh slipped and slid to the bottom of the snow-filled ravine. *Here I go again*, thought Josh as he ended up spread eagle. He could see Sheriff Daniels's huge footprints from earlier in the day but no dog tracks.

As he picked himself up and brushed off the wet snow, the whistling sounds subsided.

"That's odd," Josh thought aloud. "Maybe Flash will hear better now. Flash, Flash." He made his way farther up the ravine, paying close attention to his surroundings. That's when he heard loud grunting noises. They grew louder and closer as he stood frozen like the snowman his sister and he built earlier. Josh spun around and took off running as fast as his stocky, barrel-like legs could carry him through the drifted snow, yelling, "I'm out of here!"

Scared out of his wits and adrenaline pumping like a broken water pipe, Josh hightailed it back up the ravine toward the safe haven of the old farmhouse. He didn't stop until he reached the top of the ravine and could see the yellow stream of lights from the farmhouse.

"Flash, you're on your own. I'm headed home with or without you."

CHAPTER 19

By the time Josh reached the old white farmhouse, the night was pitch black except for the sliver of a quarter moon, and his throat felt tingly. He started coughing. Earlier in the day, his throat had a scratchy feeling like it was filled with steel wool. The annoying cough began on his return trip.

Josh turned, cupped his red chapped hands, and called one last time in the direction of the ravine, "Flash, Flash! C'mon, boy, it's time to go inside!"

Josh stood frozen like he actually was, hoping to see the familiar black head of his faithful companion appear above the ridge of the snow-covered ravine. Drifts continued to form between the ravine and the house as the snow swirled around like a whirlpool. Josh stood there for what seemed like an ongoing overtime basketball game filled with tension and excitement, but no sign of his trusted buddy emerged from the black abyss.

Josh finally pushed the back door open, exposing a yellow stream of light on the trampled backyard snow. He stepped inside the toasty house, and the door slipped from his chilled hand, slamming shut.

"What's goin' on, Josh?" asked his grandmother, standing near the stove while she poured herself a hot cup of tea.

"Flash took off running like he was after a rabbit along the ravine, and I followed him," said Josh, fighting back tears. "He went down into the ravine, and I lost sight of him. He wouldn't come back when I called him."

"He'll be back," assured his grandmother.

"I'm not so sure, Gramma. There was some funny stuff going on down in that ravine."

"Like what?"

"It's hard to explain, and I've about had all recollection scared out of me."

"You're starting to worry me, Joshua Bryan Smith."

Josh began to answer, but a deep, persistent hacking cough ensued instead.

"That's a nasty cough you have, Josh."

"Yeah, I know. My throat is killing me."

"Well, I know what to do," said his grandmother knowingly. "Go upstairs, and put on your pajamas, and I'll be right up with the Vicks."

"I was afraid of that," grumbled Josh, but he went upstairs. "I don't like how that stuff feels on my chest," complained the boy as he climbed the stairs. "It feels like little sticky pinecones on my chest."

"That may be true, but you don't sound very good, young man."

"Yeah," needled his sister, meeting him at the top of the stairs.

"Be quiet, young lady, and get away from your brother so you don't catch what he has," warned her grandmother.

"Okay."

Josh's grandmother went into his bedroom where he was sitting on the edge of his blue metal-framed bed.

"Don't look so glum, Josh, a couple of days' rests and this Vicks on your chest, and you'll be up and at 'em."

"Great with all the snow out there now."

"What happened with Sheriff Daniels?" asked his grandmother, changing the subject.

"Nothing much. He kept asking me a lot of questions, but after I showed him the skeleton, he said I could go home. He told me he couldn't do anything else until tomorrow after he contacted the Cheyenne."

"Well, I'm glad we told him and it's in his hands now. We're done with it."

"Me too."

Gramma opened the dark-blue jar of Vick's Vapor Rub and rubbed the thick, greasy, silver-looking salve on Josh's chest.

"That's cold and yucky," complained Josh as he turned to cough. "What about Flash, Gramma? You think he'll come back?"

"Sure, Josh, he's probably just chasing some rabbits. He always comes back."

"But he doesn't usually go off at night, and he acted mighty strange."

"It's just your imagination. I swear, Josh, I think all your coughing and finding that skeleton affected your brain."

"But I heard whistling noises, and I know there is a ghost out there. The crow messenger almost hit me before I came in tonight."

"There you go again. I think you're hallucinating..." bemoaned his grandmother. "But you know what Grandpa said about Cheyenne beliefs and ghosts when someone dies."

"That was the old days and ways."

"Well, I believe them because I've heard them, and where's Flash?"

"Forget the ghosts, Josh, and Flash will be back."

"But the Cheyenne believe that when a person dies—"

"Josh!"

"How do you know Flash will return this time?"

"That's enough, young man. I know what the Cheyenne believe. I was married to your grandfather for many years. That's just myths and legends."

"No, it's part of their religion, and Grandpa believed it."

"Your Grandpa was Cheyenne and kept their traditions alive."

"Well, I'm part Cheyenne, and I believe in their teachings. Besides, I had a dream about all this happening."

"There goes that imagination of yours again, Josh. Lie down and rest. I'll bring you some beef bouillon soup."

"Oh boy, I can't wait."

CHAPTER 20

After finishing his beef bouillon soup and fidgeting with the icky, sticky cotton cloth on his chest, keeping the Vicks Vapor Rub from touching his flannel pajamas, Josh fell into a deep sleep. Thoughts of Flash ran rampant in his head before he drifted off to sleep. Josh had trouble accepting the fact that Flash ran off to the ravine and didn't understand why his faithful companion wouldn't return to him when he called.

Somewhere between being awake and asleep, Josh saw Flash running in the snow toward the old Cheyenne campground along the snow-covered ravine with scattered drifts, making it hard for the athletic dog to go very fast. In his reverie, Josh caught a glimpse of Flash barking at some fast-moving, invisible creature like wind through an Oklahoma wheat field in May. When Flash approached the old Cheyenne camp where the pickup truck and skeleton were found, a large crowd began cawing overhead, sitting on the same sycamore tree as in his earlier dream, warning Josh about death and ghosts. He didn't understand the meaning of the message in this dream and wished to hear from his grandpa, but that wasn't happening at the moment.

The mysterious crow abruptly flew off, and Flash disappeared from the dream likewise. The vivid scenes within his dream were moving too fast for him to grasp, and Josh felt he was riding a gigantic merry-go-round swirling out of control with people flying off the pulsating painted horses. The carrousel spun so fast that the vibrant red, blue, yellow, green, and white colors of the horses blurred together forming a kaleidoscope.

———◆———

Thunder like a sonic boom woke Josh. He shot up in his bed soaked in sweat.

"What was that?" exclaimed Josh. He stood up and looked out the window.

Startled he fell back into bed.

"The crow," gasped Josh, "what does he want now?"

Josh sat back up on the edge of his bed and peered out the window. The black messenger sat on a tree limb outside his window and stared at him. Their eyes locked on one another.

"There go those noises again. Sounds like they're coming from the ravine," he guessed, never taking his eyes off the crow.

"Caw, caw," screeched the big bird. He flapped his wings vigorously and then flew at the window, banging it with his black beak. Josh fell back in his bed again. Without hesitation he quickly jumped up to see where the crow went, but he had disappeared in an instant.

"What does he want?" wondered Josh. "I showed Sheriff Daniels where the skeleton was. What does he want?"

Josh sat down on his bed, staring out his window. "Where's Grandpa when I need him? Where's Flash? I know where he is. He's at the old Cheyenne campground by the abandoned truck with the crow. I saw them in my dream."

The wind picked back up, and soon snow swirled outside his window like the snow on the TV when the stations went off the air for the night. The thunder stopped, and a light snow began to fall again. Some frozen limbs scraped against his frosted bedroom window, and the whistling noises rose in intensity outside his window. The crow came back and stared at Josh as if to say, "What are you waiting for? Follow me."

"I'm going to the abandoned truck right now. I've gotta find Flash. Grandmother and Caroline are asleep. I'll use Grandpa's walking stick to help me get there, and maybe the crow and ghosts won't bother me."

Josh crawled out of bed dripping with sweat like he'd been playing basketball. "My fever seems worse, but I can't worry about that now. I need to find Flash. Nobody else will."

He took off the cloth with Vicks vapor rub and changed into a clean pair of jeans and red and black checkered shirt. He quietly crept down the stairs one step at a time, stopping every once in a while, to listen for any sounds of anyone being up and moving around. But he heard none and kept on going to the kitchen. Josh headed to the back door and pulled on his cowboy boots.

"Gosh, these are still pretty wet," he said like he was talking to Flash by his side.

He quickly put on his sheepskin-lined jean jacket. *Flash would already be scratching at the back door, he thought. No noise to deal with right now until I open the door. Turn the knob slowly and steadily and pull the door back in one movement.*

Once outside Josh moved to the shed where Grandma put Grandpa's stuff. He quickly rummaged around and found his grandpa's eagle head walking stick.

Satisfied, Josh proclaimed, "This will help and keep me safe… I saw the crow so there's no telling what will happen."

He made it to the ravine. "Hope I find Flash before Grandma wakes up, and if I don't, what will she say? Who cares? I know where Flash is, and I want him to come home. I can't lose him and Grandpa both…."

"Boy, the snow is coming down harder, and the wind is picking up. It's almost like an omen. I can hear noises. They're like a human voice calling out something. Nah, maybe it's just the wind blowing," he said, trying to reassure himself.

Josh reached the point where he first saw the wild pigs. His vision blurred by the snow falling harder. He could barely see a black speck in the snow on the ground moving toward him.

"Flash, Flash, is that you? It's me, boy." Josh could hardly walk but pushed forward with the help of the walking stick. Flash barked and ran toward him.

"Did you miss me, boy? I've missed you. Why did you leave?"

Flash jumped up on him, almost knocking him over, but Josh braced himself with the walking stick. Flash turned and ran in the direction of the truck. The skeleton was still inside, and Josh wondered why.

"Wait, Flash, wait for me!" cried Josh and then heard a voice clearly.

"Find her, tell her…."

"Find who and tell her what?"

"Make it right…."

"Make what right? What's going on here?"

A chill ran through Josh like having ice water poured down his back on a warm summer day, but he still felt very hot and wanted to throw up. The snow continued to pound him, causing him to fall.

"Where's the walking stick? I've got to get out of this snowstorm." He crawled to the cab of the pickup truck, opened the door, and pulled himself up on the seat next to the skeleton not even noticing it. Josh closed the door as Flash tried to jump in with him.

"No. Flash, go and get Grandma. Go. I need help. Go, boy, and hurry."

Josh saw Flash take off running up the ravine and began to sing, "You held my hand, Grandfather, when I was very young and taught me to sing the songs that you have sung. You taught me to see, Grandfather, the things that you have seen not as they are, but as they should be. You told me the stories so I may tell my young of the strength of the bear...."

"Nahkohe, my grandson."

"Is that you, Grandfather?"

"Be brave and strong, grandson, and listen to your grandmother."

"I will, Grandfather," said Josh as he passed out, falling against the skeleton.

CHAPTER 21

The lights were on in the kitchen when Flash made it back to the house. He started barking and scratching at the back door, and Grandma let him.

"Where's Josh, Flash?" she asked with trembling in her voice. "I know he went to find you, and I know he's got a high fever. I found his sweaty clothes on his bed when I went in to check on him this morning."

Flash started barking again and pulling on her robe trying to move her to the back door.

"What is it that you want, Flash? Do you know where he is? Let me call Sheriff Daniels. I'll change my clothes and go with you."

She called Sheriff Daniels and told him about Josh being gone and Flash. "Sheriff, can you come over? I'm going with Flash to find Josh. I think he may be back down at the Cheyenne burial ground, and I think he has a bad fever and may be in trouble."

"Sure, Mrs. Smith. I'll be there in about thirty minutes. The snow has slowed down, and I can get over there pretty easy."

"I'm going to head down there and leave Caroline here for you to arrive."

"Why don't you wait for me to get there?"

"No, sheriff, with all due respect, Josh may be in trouble, and I'm going to him now. You can come down to the burial grounds when you get here."

"But Mrs. Smith…."

"No buts, Sheriff. I'm going, and that's it. I'll see you when you get there, but please hurry."

"I'm on my way."

"Flash, stay here while I go upstairs to change and wake up Caroline."

Grandma told Caroline what was happening. She was not happy about having to stay behind with all the excitement going on. She pleaded her case to Grandma but to no avail.

With that done, Grandma went downstairs and poured the leftover bullion she had on the stove into a thermos. "This will help warm Josh up when we find him. Now let's get going after that boy of ours before he dies of pneumonia."

Grandma pulled on her old black rubber boots and wrapped a scarf around her neck. She opened the back door, and Flash was out the door before she could say, "Lead the way." Instead, she yelled, "Slow down, Flash! I'm not as young as I used to be." Flash stopped and ran back to her but then took off again, heading to the ravine.

The odd pair made it to the spot where Flash and Josh first saw the wild pigs. Flash started barking, and Grandma asked, "Are we getting close, Flash?" The dog barked louder and more excitedly. "Is that a crow I hear crowing, Flash? Josh is always talking about a crow in his dreams."

Josh came to and heard the crow and voices. All kinds of voices. One sounded like his grandma calling his name. Another voice in the cab of the old truck kept saying, "Find her and tell her."

Josh bolted up like a rubber ball submerged in water, realizing he was against the skeleton, "What the heck?"

"Josh, where are you?" called Grandma as she pushed forward. She saw her husband's old walking stick on the ground and knew that her grandson must be close by.

"Grandma," called Josh, "is that you?" He tried to push the truck's rusty old door open but couldn't.

"Caw, caw," called the crow who sat in the tree above the truck and flew off when grandma reached the truck.

"Josh are you in there?" asked his grandmother.

"Yes. Are you mad that I left without telling you?"

"Why of course," said his grandmother, keeping her voice as stern as possible. "What were you thinking?"

"I know, but I had to find Flash and I had a dream…."

"Stop with the dreams, young man," snapped his grandmother. "Don't push your luck."

"I know but I'm okay…really, and Flash brought you back to me."

"I suppose. But no more of this foolishness do you hear me, Nahkohe."

If she's calling me Nahkohe, I'm okay, thought Josh. "I'm sorry for causing you to worry, Grandma. Grandpa came to me in a dream again and told me to listen to you."

"Well, maybe you should start listening to what he says. I know you miss him, and we both do. This has been a hard Christmas for all of us, our first without him and then this snowstorm and skeleton tragedy."

"I know," responded Josh.

"We'll all get through this with the help of God and knowing that Grandpa is with his Maker."

"Yeah, I know."

Sheriff Daniels arrived, shining his flashlight. The blowing snow and the light beam from the flashlight created a reflection on the truck's windshield that looked like the shape of two large teeth. Josh saw for the first time a chain hanging from the rear-view mirror with a pendant attached, made of two ivory elk teeth. Josh wondered who it belonged to, and why it was hanging there. Once again, he heard a voice from inside the truck, only this time it was a whisper, "Find her and tell her, please, Nahkohe."

Terrified, Josh pushed hard against the door, and it popped open. The sheriff was standing next to the truck and caught him before he hit the ground.

"Josh," said his grandma, "looks like you saw a ghost."

"I did or at least heard one."

"There you go again about ghosts. Your fever must be causing such notions in your head."

"But Grandma…."

"No buts. It's over and done with."

For now, thought Josh.

With Sheriff Daniels's help, they all returned to the house, and Grandma put Josh back into bed. Flash went upstairs with them and lay down beside Josh's bed.

"Good to have you home, boy, and thanks for getting Grandma."

CHAPTER 22

Before Josh knew it, school was almost ready to resume, with him spending most of his time in bed while the snow was still on the ground. Raising temperatures caused the snow to melt quite quickly. Temperatures in Oklahoma rarely stayed low for long periods of time. The front-yard Frosty looked like the last bite of ice cream before actually eating the cone itself. His aunts and uncles all finally made it by to exchange gifts once Josh's fever broke and his coughed subsided. The two uncles came at different times with their families. The atmosphere didn't feel like Christmas but more like a Sunday afternoon visit. The visits felt more like an obligation, which disappointed Josh's grandmother, who preferred having all her children and grandchildren together for a festive celebration where she fed them her home-cooked meals and spoiled her grandkids.

An unexpected knock came on the front door just before the sun went down one afternoon. Gramma opened the door, and Sheriff Daniels filled the doorway, removing his white Stetson.

"How are you doin', Sheriff?" asked Gramma as she invited him in and led him into the kitchen.

"Just fine, Mrs. Smith, now that the weather has let up. Thanks for asking. What about yourself?"

"Things are lookin' up with my grandson startin' to feel better."

Gramma had meat-and-potato pies in the oven, an old Irish recipe of hers. They were one of Josh's favorites. Their aroma filled the house and was enticing enough to kill for the chance to have a taste.

"Do you want a cup of coffee and a piece of pie, Sheriff?" asked Grandma whose blue eyes looked livelier than ever.

"What kind of pie?" inquired the sheriff as he put his cowboy hat on the coat rack hanging next to the back door.

"Meat n' potato," volunteered Caroline, who'd just entered the kitchen seeking a piece for herself like a heat-seeking missile.

"No, I think I'll pass if it's all right with you, Mrs. Smith, but I'll take that cup of coffee."

Gramma looked surprised the big man passed up her meat-n'-potato pie, but it wasn't all that common in this part of the country.

"You don't know what you're missing, Sheriff. It's mighty good," commented Caroline. "I believe I'll have some myself."

"No, you won't, missy, not until it's suppertime," said Gramma emphatically while she poured Sheriff Daniels a steaming hot cup of coffee. That's the way her late husband liked it. Steam rose from the cup as the ebony liquid went into the green jadeite cup.

That's how she liked serving all her hot drinks.

Leaning back in his chair, Sheriff Daniels held his cup to his mouth with both his enormous hands that were the size of bear paws. His fingers looked like bratwurst. He blew on the walnut-colored coffee and savored the fresh aroma.

"How's that dog of your grandson's doing?" asked the sheriff after taking a sip of his coffee and placing the cup back down on the table.

Before Gramma could answer, Flash and Josh meandered into the kitchen. "He's okay, Sheriff," answered the pleased but anxious boy.

"He doesn't run off anymore. Are you here to tell us about the skeleton in the truck?"

"As a matter fact, I am, son. We were able to identify the truck from the Texas plates that were on it. We found who it was registered to from an FBI missing person's list."

"Who was it?" asked an anxious Josh.

"Take it easy, Josh," said the sheriff with a chuckle. "We will get to that in due time."

"Okay, sir. I'm just excited to put this all to rest."

"I understand, Josh. The skeleton was an older gentleman who had a steel pin in his left leg from a bad fall he took down a flight of stairs a few years ago. They used a steel pin because of his age."

"That was too bad for him," said Gramma, listening intently while straightening up the kitchen.

"Wow, a steel pin in his leg," yelled Caroline. "Gross."

"What's so gross about that?" asked Josh.

"It just is."

Sheriff Daniels sat patiently amused by the banter between Josh and his sister.

"I think you have a steel pin in your head," retorted Josh.

"Stop your fussing, you two," scolded Gramma, "and, you, young man, should know better because you're older."

"Okay," agreed Josh.

"If you don't start acting older, you can forget about using that new twenty-two you got for Christmas. It will stay in the box until you do," warned his grandmother.

"Maybe we can go out and shoot it together some time," suggested Sheriff Daniels.

"Sounds great," said Josh.

Gramma turned her attention to Caroline. "You, young lady, go upstairs and pick up your room."

"Do I have to?" whined Caroline.

Gramma gave her typical I-mean-business look.

Caroline quickly got up from the table and went upstairs, but before she did, she looked cross-eyed at her brother, knowing that his grandmother was watching him, and he was in no position to retaliate.

Before she made it to the stairs, Caroline gave one last effort at staying downstairs. "Why does Josh get to stay?"

"Because what Sheriff Daniels has to tell us involves Josh. Now get up those stairs pronto."

"But he always gets to stay," complained Caroline as she stomped up the stairs with her curls bouncing up and down like popping embers in the fireplace.

The gentle giant during all of this looked like the proverbial cat that swallowed the bird and even turned his head away once in an effort to stifle one of his typical jolly, belly shaking laughs. He didn't succeed, but fortunately Caroline was out of sight.

"I apologize, Sheriff Daniels, for the rude behavior of my grandchildren."

"That's okay, Mrs. Smith. I have young children of my own."

"Children!" exclaimed Gramma, "Sometimes I just don't know what to do with them."

Sheriff Daniels finally spoke up again, returning to the reason for his visit. "It appears the driver of the truck was in the early stages of Alzheimer's and just drove off one day from the family ranch in Texas. He must have gotten lost and didn't know where he was. The family reported him missing back in March, but no one had any idea where he went. They didn't even realize he was missing for a while on the day he left. It wasn't unusual for him to drive off on their large ranch, but he always managed to find his way back."

"So how did he end up in the ravine?" asked Josh.

"Apparently the old gent suffered a massive heart attack, and that's what caused him to drive off the road and down into the ravine."

"No one saw it happen?" exclaimed Josh's grandmother.

"It probably happened late at night because the light switch to his headlights was still pulled out."

"Well, that's too bad. I feel sorry for his family not knowing where he was for so long and then not being with him at the end. We know what it is to lose a loved one."

Gramma looked over at Josh and smiled sheepishly as she straightened her well- worn blue gingham apron.

"Do you want some more coffee, Sheriff?" asked Gramma.

"No, thanks. I need to be heading back to the station. Thought I'd check to see how you were doing and figured you might be wondering about the skeleton."

The sheriff pushed his chair back and stood up. "You make a fine cup of coffee, Mrs. Smith." The Jolly Green Giant sheriff reached for his Stetson.

"You probably tell all the women that, Harry Daniels. You know how to charm the womenfolk," Gramma said with a rare smile since the recent passing of her longtime husband. She opened the door for the sheriff as he ducked his head and stepped out on to the front porch.

The sun was high in the sky above him, shining brightly. "Looks like we're going to have a nice day."

"Sure does," said Gramma, "and thanks for checking on Josh and Flash and telling us about the skeleton."

"You're welcome and tell Caroline to go easy on her brother."

"I heard that," said Josh, moving in behind Gramma at the front door. "Yes, I wanted to know about the skeleton. Thanks, and I'll take you up on your offer to go out and shoot my twenty-two soon. If we do, Gramma will probably let me use it sooner."

"That's a deal," said Sheriff Daniels as he tipped his hat to Gramma.

"Thanks, Sheriff, and have a good day," said Gramma as she closed the door. Gramma turned toward Josh. "Well, I'm relieved to know that it was an accident, and no foul play involved with the man's death."

"Me too," agreed Josh.

EPILOGUE

The following summer Josh received an unexpected phone call from the wife of the man who died in the crashed pickup, thanking him for finding her husband and informing the proper authorities. She asked if she might come some weekend and have Josh show her exactly where her husband died. Josh and his grandmother agreed. In the spring, Josh and his grandmother placed a small white cross to mark the spot where Josh found the pickup and skeleton after they received permission from the Cheyenne elders in El Reno.

That summer, the widow visited Josh and his grandmother. She and his grandmother talked a long time before they all went out to see the sight, as Josh's grandmother and the widow had a lot in common, for they both had experienced the loss of their husbands in the same year. Josh remarked to his grandmother that the lady was younger looking than he expected and seemed to be in good spirits having lost her husband in such a surprising and gruesome way. His grandmother agreed and told him that people had different ways in dealing with loss and grief and each had their own timetable in moving through it. Some people never do; they all had, but Josh still wondered about the two ivory elk teeth pendant that he saw that last night, and who he was supposed to find, and what he was supposed to tell her.

BACKMATTER

Josh gulped hard, trying to catch his breath. "What's that, boy?"
Flash barked but didn't look back at his master.
"I don't remember seeing that truck there before now."
Flash's curiosity finally took over, and he sprinted toward the
snow-covered blue pickup. The door windows were down, and the
front windshield was shattered into a sea- green mosaic of a
thousand pieces....
"Is that what I think it is, Flash? Is that a bone hanging out of the
window?"

On a snowy, Oklahoma Christmas Eve, Josh and his dog, Flash, happen upon a skeleton in an old pickup on the Cheyenne campground—an area Josh isn't allowed to visit. When Grandpa was alive, he told Josh the Cheyenne legends, including the one about ghosts who weren't properly buried. Grandpa would know what to do about the skeleton, but he's not here anymore, and Grandma doesn't believe in the Cheyenne stories.

Josh continues to be haunted by ghosts, memories of Grandpa, and the mysterious black crow who seems to be telling him something. Then one night Flash runs away, and

Josh must confront all of his biggest fears. Will Josh be able to do the right thing? Find out in Josh and the Skeleton.

Skip Ashworth is an award-winning teacher and coach, working with students in fifth grade through college for forty-nine plus years. He developed his own Oklahoma history course for which he received an award for Excellence in Teaching Oklahoma History.

The author enjoys learning about and participating in the Chickasaw culture with his wife who is part Chickasaw herself.